worth Waiting For

OTHER BOOKS BY SALLY JOHNSON

The Skeleton in My Closet Wears a Wedding Dress

worth

Waiting

a novel

For

SALLY JOHNSON

Covenant Communications, Inc.

Cover: *Woman on Railroad Station Platform* © pidjoe. Courtesy of istockphoto.com

Cover design copyright © 2015 by Covenant Communications, Inc.

Published by Covenant Communications, Inc.
American Fork, Utah

Printed in the United States of America
First Printing: July 2015

21 20 19 18 17 16 15   10 9 8 7 6 5 4 3 2 1

ISBN: 979-1-68047-240-0

To my husband, Steve,
for encouraging me to keep writing.
And to my kids,
for letting me write.

Acknowledgments

THANK YOU (AGAIN) TO TRISHA Luong, Micheal Evon, and Janna MacKay for reading and rereading, making suggestions, and giving advice. And thank you to Jean Wong, Anna Trout, Tamara Seiter, and Meghan Jacobsen—my own little tribe.

(As Always), thank you so much to my editor, Samantha Millburn. I appreciate everything you do for me and especially all the questions you answer, because I know I ask a lot.

Chapter One
No Way!

ELOPE?

What?

Really?

I wasn't sure I had heard correctly.

"They eloped! They eloped!" my roommate Rhonda Jesop screamed, bounding up the stairs toward our apartment, waving her cell phone. She could be heard from three flights below at the end of the hall in our complex and probably around the world. I assumed she was directing her screams at me, but I wasn't sure. I looked around to see if there was anyone else she could have been yelling to. I kind of hoped there was.

I was coming back from the mailbox, and we arrived at our apartment almost simultaneously. Our other roommate Sarah Sellers opened the front door, obviously hearing Rhonda's ruckus, which would have been hard to miss.

"They got married," Rhonda panted, bending over with her hands on her knees, trying to catch her breath from her breakneck sprint up the stairs. Her long brown curls hung over her face.

"Who?" I reviewed in my mind the people we knew who were getting married. Most of the invitations we had received had dates coinciding with the immediate end of the semester.

"Claire and Travis," she managed, still sounding winded.

"Claire and Travis?" I repeated stupidly. Claire and Travis? They had just gotten engaged. We—or at least Rhonda and Sarah, because I knew I wouldn't be getting one—hadn't even gotten an invitation yet. My ex-husband had suddenly run off and married my ex-roommate? "I need to sit down," I announced, stepping into the kitchen and finding the first chair I could. It was bad enough I already had an ex-husband at nineteen years old, but my ex-husband and my ex-roommate eloping? *Really?* I kind of thought, assumed, and secretly hoped, they would never last long enough to make it to the altar.

"No way." Sarah got her deer-in-the-headlights look: her blue eyes wide open, mouth gaping in surprise. She slid into the chair across from me and smoothed her thick, blonde hair away from her face several times in a row.

"What?" Rhonda's BFF and our temporary roommate, Ashlee Lowe, walked into the room, carrying her loaded bag from hairdressing school and easily joining the conversation about the shocking news.

"Claire and Travis eloped," Rhonda blurted. She almost sounded excited.

Sarah was still visibly shaken. "Are you sure?"

I was surprised she would question Rhonda's information. Rhonda seemed to know everything about everyone. Her word was like the bible of gossip—I mean, pertinent, must-know information that involved us all. So *technically* we weren't gossiping.

Ashlee dropped her bag on the floor and sat down beside me. "Seriously?" She drew the word out in disbelief. She was a cute, petite girl from Texas, so when she talked slowly, her accent was more pronounced.

Rhonda waved her cell phone in the air. "I went over last night to talk to her, and her roommates said she wasn't home, so I called her. She called me back today and left a message. Oh my gosh! Listen."

We huddled together to hear the message on speaker. "Rhonda. Claire. I'm returning your call. Travis and I went to Vegas . . . and got married!"

I might have detected a small note of excitement at the end when she announced they got married, but I wasn't sure. Claire rarely got excited about anything and hardly ever showed any emotion. Well, warm emotion. And she certainly never did what I expected.

Like marry my ex-husband—that was unexpected. Or even date my ex-husband, for that matter. That was unexpected. And her *eloping?* That was *very* unexpected. And doing it in Vegas. That was beyond unexpected.

"She's joking, right?" Sarah sounded more worried than happy.

Rhonda and I both gave her a look of *Don't be ridiculous.* "Have you ever known Claire to joke?" I asked. Secretly I kept hoping maybe it was an early April Fool's Day joke, though the last time I hoped that, it wasn't. The previous April Fool's Day, Travis announced he wanted a divorce. And

Claire and Travis eloping as an April Fool's Day joke would be too easy an explanation in my complicated life.

"No, but . . ." Sarah paused. "Wouldn't she have wanted to get married in the temple? They could have at least eloped there." Sarah had just called off her own wedding, and she sounded disappointed in Claire's decision.

"They could have, I guess, instead of going to a little church on Las Vegas Boulevard. That's what I'd want to do if I were inclined to elope," I said.

"So if you and Luke got married . . ." Rhonda hinted.

I blushed. Luke and I. I liked the way that sounded. Not the marry part, though, because we had just recently started dating and I couldn't let my mind go *there* yet. Actually, I didn't *want* my mind to go there yet. I had been swept off my feet and then kicked to the curb once before. I was not making a mistake like that again. Ever.

"Let's not jump to conclusions too quickly. I don't want to be rash like Travis. Besides, Luke is going to Europe for spring term, so there are no plans to elope."

"Isn't that the point of eloping?" Ashlee asked. "It's not planned?"

"Yeah, but what Claire and Travis did was crazy," I continued, starting to sound like I was ranting. "I mean, who knew Travis was going to find his next true love so quickly? It hasn't even been an official year since he left me."

"Speaking of leaving you . . ." Rhonda got a hungry look in her eyes—hungry for information I hadn't fully given her yet. Information she'd been dying to know since the big discovery six weeks before that I, in fact, had been married *and* divorced my first year at BYU. Busy year.

I brought the conversation around to the matter that was really at hand. "No, no. We're not speaking of me; we're speaking of Claire's crazy announcement."

"It was definitely quick," Ashlee noted. "My dad would kill me."

"For eloping?" I asked.

"For getting married so young, so quickly."

"Even in the temple?" Rhonda added.

"Especially in the temple," Ashlee said.

Ashlee's comment seemed strange to me, but I didn't ask her about it. I was still gobsmacked by the idea of Claire eloping. "Who would have thought she'd elope? So rash. So . . . unplanned." I kept voicing the thoughts running through my head. Claire never ceased to amaze me. And that wasn't always a good thing.

This elopement was crazy on so many levels. She was an accounting major. She liked everything in her life to be like a spreadsheet. Checks and balances. This included decisions. She was organized and meticulous and anal and methodical. Eloping was crazy, impulsive and unplanned, unorganized and way too spur-of-the-moment for Claire, who lived for her schedule. But Travis, he was a different story.

Travis could flash his smile, melt every female heart in the room, and have every male convinced he was a good guy. He was *that* good. He was beautiful, gorgeous, charming, and convincing all at the same time. I should know. I had once been under his spell. And no, I was not in love with him anymore; that all came with objectivity, not bias. And it was all true. But that was all he had: his looks and his charm. He had no shame. His only concern was what made *him* happy. He had no regrets for the destruction he left in his wake of selfish choices and never looked back to view his handiwork. What Travis wanted, Travis got and usually whenever he wanted.

Apparently he wanted Claire to be his wife, and he wanted it now.

Presumably his parents were not in on his little decision to run off to Vegas and get married because Vegas was not on his mother's list of approved cities. Travis's mother, Maxine Duckk, abhorred with a passion the city of Las Vegas and all the sin that dwelled therein. I, on the other hand, grew up in Las Vegas and loved it.

But enough wasted time on thoughts of them. I would much rather dwell on the implications this irresponsible decision would reap. Ha! Travis would have to face the wrath of his mother. I would rather have a tooth pulled without Novocain than deal with an unhappy Maxine. I still couldn't fathom it. Vegas? Eloping? *Really?* Travis would have to live with Claire, and even I would not wish that on my worst enemy. Oh, wait. Travis was my worst enemy, and I didn't even have to wish it on him; he'd already brought it upon himself. See, there *was* justice in the world. Who said the Lord didn't answer prayers?

Chapter Two
To Go or Not to Go? That Is the Question

RHONDA, BEING A SELF-PROCLAIMED Martha Stewart/Rachael Ray hybrid, didn't hesitate to jump in and offer to throw Claire a bridal shower, ignoring the minor detail that she was *already* married. Any excuse to bake food and gather people together was good enough for Rhonda. Never mind Ashlee was right there agreeing with her. Not that we didn't have enough to worry about with finals fast approaching, Sarah's funk over her broken engagement, and the end-of-the-semester apartment cleaning.

"Are they already back from their honeymoon?" I asked, curious. I knew I shouldn't care and that curiosity killed the cat, but I couldn't help it. Obviously, if I were a cat, I'd be dead.

"Claire said there wasn't time and they're waiting until after the semester to go."

"Are they going on a cruise?"

Rhonda seemed surprised. "How'd you know?"

Been there, done that, I thought. "Just guessing," I said to Rhonda. "I'm surprised you're able to squeeze in a shower before the end of the semester."

"I think it's important," Rhonda said. After a moment she asked, "Are you sure you're okay with us doing it?" Rhonda was cautious about where I stood on the matter, but she felt it was her roommate duty to throw Claire a shower, and as a roommate, I was invited to help with the happy, festive occasion.

"You're not including me in the 'us', are you?" I didn't consider myself *that* okay with it. I didn't want to help plan it. I didn't want to help throw it. The only thing I felt like throwing was *up*. I would have loved to attend, but only if I could be a fly on the wall. Just to witness it. But, really, did I want to go? Did I not want to go? That was the question. I definitely did *not* want to go if Travis was going to be there.

"I was thinking more of me, Sarah . . . and Ashlee." It was still unclear whether we should group Ashlee in with the roommates since she and Claire had switched apartments last month. "You can if you want." Rhonda shrugged. "I didn't know how you would feel about it."

I snorted. "You don't need my permission."

Rhonda paused. "But it'd be weird throwing Claire a shower as her roommates and not including you. But we also thought it'd be weird asking you to help because she married your ex-husband."

I waved a dismissive hand. "I don't care if you throw it. I'm not going to help you though." But I did kind of care. I only said that because I thought that was what my answer *should* be. It still burned me that Travis ran off and married the girl. But being bitter and vindictive was not very attractive behavior, so I was attempting to be as diplomatic as possible, though I was still trying to figure out how exactly I was going to accomplish *that*.

"We kind of assumed you wouldn't be helping. But you are invited, you know. You were her roommate. Just because she married your ex-husband doesn't mean she has to be your arch enemy."

If only I could embrace that attitude.

* * *

I was busy making chicken pasta salad the night before the shower when Rhonda, Ashlee, and Sarah came in the front door carrying grocery bags.

Rhonda eyed my bowl of pasta as I was stirring in the last of the ingredients. "Is that for tomorrow?" She looked puzzled.

"Yes. But . . ."

"Can I try some?" Rhonda interrupted.

"Sure." I pushed the bowl toward her, surprised she wanted a sample. Rhonda prided herself on being the food guru of the apartment. She was usually making the food, not trying other people's.

"This is really good. You made it?"

"Yes."

"Really?" She looked at me suspiciously.

"Yeah. Why?" I'm sure her suspicion stemmed from last semester when I never cooked.

"You didn't buy this at Smith's?"

"You think I went to the grocery store and bought five pounds of pasta salad?" I was pretty sure they'd just come from there since all their grocery bags read Smith's. Did she think she saw me at the deli?

"Yeah."

"No, it is just one of those rare occasions when I cooked."

Rhonda chewed thoughtfully. "We don't know how many are coming for the shower, but I think that will be enough."

"This isn't for the shower," I corrected her. "I'm going to Luke's for lunch." I thought for a moment. "The shower's not here, right? Isn't it at the clubhouse?"

"Yeah." Sarah started putting away the food. "We didn't want it to be uncomfortable for you."

"So that's not for us?" Rhonda repeated, pointing at the salad. She seemed disappointed.

"No, sorry." I dismissed myself from the kitchen as they busied themselves prepping for tomorrow's party. All this effort just to celebrate the love of Travis and Claire. I hated the happy couple. Maybe hate was too strong a word. Or not strong enough.

* * *

The next day I surreptitiously watched the preparations for the bridal shower taking place in the clubhouse in the courtyard of our apartment building. I deliberated a lot about going to the shower. I didn't want to be there, but I did. I didn't really like Claire, and I liked her a whole lot less now that she was married to Travis. And what if Travis was there? I didn't want to see him. Talk about uncomfortable. But then there was the curiosity factor. I mean, they ran off and got married. Were they really married? I kind of wanted to see for myself. I had a sick sense of curiosity I wanted to satisfy but didn't know if I was brave enough to show up. I kept reminding myself that curiosity killed the cat.

A knock on the door interrupted my contemplations and spying. I opened it to a girl from downstairs holding a gift.

"Hey, you're that girl," she said.

I was confused. Did she think I was Claire? "I'm sorry, who?"

"The Barbie doll girl. That's what all my roommates call you."

I considered what she'd said. I knew she was commenting on my looks, but I didn't know what the proper response was. It was something I had heard all my life. I was 5'10" and had long blonde hair, green eyes, a pert nose, and full lips, but my life had been far from *Life in the Dreamhouse*, even though I looked like the doll.

The girl ignored my lack of response. "Is the shower here?"

"The clubhouse." I looked in that direction.

"Oh, sorry. Aren't you going?"

I shook my head quickly. "No, I am *not* going."

The girl seemed puzzled but said, "Thanks," and headed toward the party.

I continued my spying. To me, it was like passing by a car accident or, in more appropriately monumental proportions, a train wreck—I just had to look. I *wanted* to look. I had to witness the catastrophe. But in the end, my curiosity was satisfied by a weird twist of fate, and I sort of had to go.

I didn't expect pasta salad would be what got me there, but before I even had a chance to go to Luke's for lunch, Rhonda called me. She sounded frantic. "Sophia, we have a problem."

"What?" I asked cautiously. Did *we* have the problem, or did *she* have the problem?

"Claire invited like fifteen extra people she didn't tell us about, and I don't think we have enough food. Could we maybe borrow your pasta salad and then replace it later? Please?"

Two things very important to Rhonda were preparation and presentation. She wanted a great spread of food, and she wanted it to look great. Not having enough food would make her feel unprepared and panicked.

I was surprised Claire would even have fifteen people to invite. I'd never found her particularly friendly, and I'd never seen her with any friends. The only place she ever went that I knew about was her brother's house. But then again, she did manage to date and get engaged to my ex-husband without my knowing it.

"I guess so," I said slowly, having the reality of showing up at Claire's bridal shower sink in. "I'll be down in a few minutes." I needed some time to psych myself up for this. To *prepare* myself.

Anticipation, trepidation, apprehension—I was a whole thesaurus of nervous. I held on to my bowl of pasta salad like it was a life vest, both fearful and excited as I paced my steps down to the clubhouse. I stopped to gather my thoughts and emotions before opening the door. *Okay, I can do this. If I don't act nervous, no one will know I am nervous. If I smile and act happy, people will think I am happy. I can be the bigger person. I am over Travis. I have Luke. I am happy. I am happier now than I was with Travis. Travis and Claire deserve each other. I can do this. I can do this. I can do this*. Maybe if I said it enough times in my mind, I would actually believe it. I took a deep breath and walked in.

Claire was all aglow. Married life must have been good for her so far. Maybe all she needed was love. Isn't that what the Beatles said?

I set the bowl down on the food table and checked out the party. There was actually a decent turnout. I supposed she had to have friends. Maybe from high school? Maybe from college classes? Former roommates? Visiting teachers? Although I didn't think she was ever home to have them come over. Maybe they met her up at the library or the Cougareat or some other place on campus since campus was her other home.

I was also surprised to see Maxine, my ex-mother-in-law, there in all her bottle-redhead beauty, her helmet hair big and solid. Somehow I'd forgotten my ex-mother-in-law might be in attendance. I hadn't seen her since before the divorce. I could tell by the expression that passed over her face, ever so briefly, she had not been expecting to see me either. She had always been intimidating, and I'd felt like she'd never approved of me. I'd known we would never be close when she told me she was the most important woman in her son's life and I needed to accept that.

Her being there added to my nervousness. I could avoid her like the plague and hope our paths didn't cross, or I could seize the day and deal with her straight on. I hadn't come here looking for revenge, but I was not going to let her get the better of me this time. Besides, what did it matter? She wasn't my mother-in-law anymore. I didn't need to make nice or impress her. And hopefully I would never have to see her again.

"Maxine," I said with all the neutrality I could muster.

"Fifi?" She called me by the nickname Travis always used.

"Uh, it's Sophia. I'm not Fifi anymore."

"What are you doing here?" I could hear the disdain in her voice.

"Celebrating Claire's elopement. Isn't that why you're here?"

"You're friends with Claire?"

I bobbed my head, deciding how to answer. "I wouldn't say friends. More like roommates. But now that she's married my ex-husband, I'm not sure what it'd be called. Frenemies?"

"Maybe this time the marriage will last." Maxine gave me a sort of sideways half glance, then looked straight ahead.

Many things ran through my head I would have loved to say, but they would only reflect badly on me, and I knew it was not becoming. Instead, I looked directly at her and said, "I wasn't the one who changed my mind."

Maxine didn't reply. She just turned and walked away from me.

I was pleased I had handled her in a mature way until I looked up to see Claire staring at me with a look of death. It brought me back to the reality of the situation and quickly eliminated the smile on my face. Maybe I wouldn't be sticking around too long. Maybe just long enough to grab a plate of food. To go.

While making my way across the room, I overheard part of a conversation. I assumed the person talking was a friend of Claire's, but since I didn't know Claire had any friends, I couldn't be sure. Maybe the sister-in-law married to the brother I had never met.

"I'm so excited for Claire. Were you so happy when you heard the news? Eloping. How romantic."

"Not exactly the wedding I wanted for my only daughter," a woman who could only be Claire's mother replied. She had a note of contempt in her voice and sat ramrod straight, just like her daughter.

So Claire's mom wasn't happy about the elopement. It made me think of how unhappy Maxine had been with my marriage to Travis. It made me appreciate that I had gotten out when I did.

As luck would have it, Maxine was at the food table when I arrived. "Did you cook this?" Maxine asked, pointing to her plate. Her finger hovered above my chicken salad.

"Just that chicken salad," I said, loading my plate with food. I watched as Maxine immediately tossed her plate of untouched salad in the trash. I guessed she was still afraid of my cooking.

Claire marched over to me. "What are you doing here?"

All the bravado I had with Maxine dissipated quickly. "I'm your roommate. And . . . pasta salad." My voice sounded a little shaky, and I worried about stuttering.

It was not so much that I was afraid of Claire, because I wasn't. I was uncomfortable with Claire, especially since she'd married Travis. My feelings were totally understandable, I tried to convince myself.

She glared at me. "I don't want you here."

How could I argue with that? Besides, I really didn't want to be there anymore. "Okay." I turned to leave but grabbed a couple croissants and two more spoonfuls of chicken pasta salad to go. After all, it was mine.

My heart thudded as I headed for the door, feeling the weight of everyone in the room staring at me. I gripped my plate tighter and hurried to Luke's apartment to recover.

"Hey there," Luke said, his voice all warm and creamy as he opened the door. He gave me a kiss on the forehead before letting me in. "Are you bringing me lunch?" His smile reached all the way up to his hazel eyes.

"I got kicked out of Claire's bridal shower," I said, plopping down at his kitchen table. He sat down next to me and ran his hand through his brown hair but said nothing. He was probably waiting for the rest of the story.

"Do you want some of this?" I asked, motioning toward the food as I started to dig in.

He took the forkful I was holding and redirected it to his mouth. "Mmm. That's good," he murmured as he chewed. The little act of his sharing food struck me as intimate. I liked it.

He got himself a fork. "Did you really want to be there? At the shower, I mean?" He took another bite.

"No. Yes. I don't know. I don't care, but I do. Maybe it was just curiosity. You know, like I had to see if she was *really* married. I don't know."

"And?"

"She was there, ring and all, glowing with marital bliss." I filled the croissants with salad.

"Okay."

"Maxine was there." I took a bite of my sandwich.

"Who?" Luke looked up, clueless.

I had to swallow before I could answer. "My ex-mother-in-law."

"Did she talk to you?"

"Actually, I went up and talked to her. She's a lot less intimidating when I'm not married to her son and don't feel like I have to make her like me."

"Sophia?"

I stopped. "What?"

"Did you make this pasta salad?" He pointed down at it with his fork.

I panicked. "Don't worry, the chicken is completely cooked." Luke knew about the Thanksgiving turkey I'd undercooked that had given my ex-in-laws food poisoning.

"That's not why I was wondering. It's really good."

I smiled.

"Who cares about your nasty old ex-mother-in-law and your ex-husband and your ex-roommate when you can make food this good?" He leaned over to kiss me.

"Hey. Hey." Luke's best friend and roommate, Justin, came into the kitchen. "None of that, you closet lovebirds. Or should I say, laundry-room lovebirds?"

"You're just jealous." I rolled my eyes at Justin. But I couldn't help smiling. He was always funny.

"That's right. I wish I could meet a beautiful girl in the laundry room. I would be interested and dedicated about doing my laundry every week."

"You never know when you're going to meet that girl." Luke's eyes slid over to me.

"Who's that food for?" Justin was always hungry too. "Luke's birthday isn't until next week."

"Your birthday's next week?" I looked at Luke in surprise. That was something I didn't know about him.

He shrugged. "Yeah, the twelfth."

I committed it to memory.

"Are you going to bring food next week too?" Justin asked, taking a seat.

"We'll see. Rhonda might go into shock if I cook twice in one week." Luke chuckled.

"Do you want a sandwich?" I offered Justin the croissant, which he willingly took.

"Where'd this come from? Is there a ward activity?"

I gave a toothy smile. "No, no. Just Claire's bridal shower."

Justin chewed slowly, looking thoughtful. "I wonder if I could score some more sandwiches."

"Only if you're willing to brave the shower." I looked out the window at the clubhouse.

Justin followed my gaze. "I'd have to think of a good excuse."

"You could wait until it's over and offer to help clean up," I suggested.

"What if they run out of food?"

I didn't realize he was serious. "You're really considering crashing the bridal shower just to get some food?"

"This is good." Justin held up his sandwich as if defending his motive.

"I'll give you five bucks to do it," Luke challenged Justin, pulling a five dollar bill from the front pocket of his jeans.

I pictured Justin strutting in there, and I started laughing. "You could say you're the entertainment."

Justin looked at me. "And do what, Sophia?"

"I don't know. You were the cheerleader in high school."

"That was to pick up girls, remember?"

"Can't you make up some cheer? You know, 'Travis and Claire, Travis and Claire, you are crazy, we declare!' or something, do the splits and take a bow? Then you could ask for a drink, claiming all that exercise left you parched, and help yourself to some food. You might even be able to pull it off."

"I'll give you an extra five bucks if you do the cheer," Luke said, laughing.

Justin agreed. "You come up with a better cheer, and I'll do it."

Less than five minutes later, Luke and I stared out the window as Justin sauntered into the clubhouse. A few minutes later, he returned with a plate of food and a huge smile. "You owe me ten bucks," he said, taking a bite. "I said I was a singing telegram."

"You really did it?"

"Ask Rhonda. I think they were all very entertained and shocked, but very entertained." Justin grinned. "And who's the cougar wannabe with the red hair?" He looked out the window and pointed. Maxine was standing outside the clubhouse, talking to someone.

"The what?" Luke strained to look out the window from his chair. "Is Cosmo there?"

"That lady there who's like sixty years old but dresses like she thinks she's in college."

Maxine was only in her late forties. She would have been so offended if she'd heard someone thought she looked twenty years older.

"Maxine—Claire's new mother-in-law," I supplied.

Justin shook his head and chewed his food. "That is insane, Claire eloping like that."

"But we got some really good pasta salad out of the deal," Luke piped up.

Justin paused midbite. "You guys aren't going to do anything like that, are you?"

I blushed but didn't answer immediately. I knew the answer was an emphatic no, but I didn't want to send the wrong message to Luke. I liked him— a lot—but being in love and getting married were sore spots in our relationship since I was afraid to go there. Not that we were anywhere near that point.

"Nope, no plans to hit Vegas," Luke said easily, still eating.

I let out the breath I hadn't realized I'd been holding. If I said "I love you" out loud, there was no turning back. There were witnesses and responsibility and accountability. It was like starting a diet. If I didn't tell anyone I was dieting, no one would know if I didn't lose any weight and completely failed at the diet. I wouldn't be held accountable. It was the same thing with love. Surely he had to know how I felt. Did I actually have to say those words for him to understand how much I cared about him?

"Wait. You guys aren't already married secretly, are you?" Justin raised an eyebrow. "Everything has been very hush-hush with you two." Then he smirked. "Doing laundry. I should have known."

"I'm barely divorced, Justin," I said.

"And so was your ex-husband."

And how could I answer that? Anything I said would be an immediate reflection on my feelings and attitude toward Luke. But that wasn't necessarily the case. I wasn't against getting remarried, and hopefully someday I would, but I was not going to rush into anything. Not with Luke, not with anybody.

Chapter Three
Imminent Proposal

I HATED WHEN A BOYFRIEND had a birthday. I never knew what to give him. I had to consider every possibility of the message conveyed by the gift. Did it suggest too much, like, "I hope you ask me to marry you?" Or did it seem like I didn't care, like, "Here, have a pen I just bought at the bookstore five minutes ago"? Any gift could be misconstrued into meaning too much or not enough. Basically what it came down to was I didn't know what to get Luke for his birthday.

The next time Luke was over, I brought the subject up. "Do you want me to cook dinner for you on your birthday?" We were sitting at the kitchen table eating the cookies Rhonda had just taken out of the oven.

Behind me, Rhonda snickered.

"What?" I turned to face her. "I can cook. I'm not as domestically challenged as you think. I cooked the whole time I was married. And don't forget the food prep class I am currently taking."

Rhonda raised an eyebrow. She still didn't believe me, but I didn't let it bother me. My life and self-esteem did not depend on whether or not I could cook. My goal in life was not to be the next Martha Stewart or Rachael Ray.

"Nah," Luke interrupted. "I have something else I want to do."

Rhonda's eyes almost popped out of her head, her eyebrows seemingly stuck in raised position. Her mouth gaped open.

I turned back to Luke. "So you want to take care of the plans?" I clarified.

"Yeah, if that's okay."

"Sure, sure," I said, relieved to be off the hook.

Rhonda about went ballistic when he left. "Oh. My. Gosh. Do you think he's going to propose?" I'm sure she screamed it loud enough that Luke could hear her. He had barely shut the door.

I scowled. "No." Then I added an emphatic shake of my head. "I doubt it. We're not at that point yet."

"What do you mean 'at that point yet'?" Rhonda asked. "You two have a romantic relationship that seems to be heading in the direction of—"

"La la la la. I don't want to hear it," I broke in, sticking my fingers in my ears. "Don't say it."

"You might not want to admit it, but I wouldn't be surprised." Rhonda looked put out. Maybe she was annoyed that my relationship was at a point she wanted her relationship with my brother, Dan, to be at. She had been in a long-distance relationship with him since February. He was living at home with my parents in Las Vegas, having graduated from BYU the year before and taken a job close to home.

In order to avoid any further discussion, I escaped to Luke's apartment. "Rhonda is not shutting up about you planning your birthday night," I said as he opened the door and I walked in.

Luke grinned. "I would rather take you out to dinner and spend the evening alone in a dark restaurant."

If I relayed that information to Rhonda, she would surely think a proposal was imminent.

"You really don't want me to plan anything?"

"Just plan on spending the evening with me." He played with my fingertips.

"Can I at least bake you a cake? A chocolate chocolate chip Bundt cake?" I asked, trying to tempt him. What Rhonda had said earlier was starting to worry me. It didn't seem usual to make your own birthday plans. Unless, of course, you were Rhonda. She had planned her last birthday party as a surprise party, but we'd all ended up going out to eat instead. That was the night she and my brother had first laid eyes on each other, instantly hit it off, and been virtually dating ever since.

Luke laced his fingers with mine. "That would be great. I'd love that."

"So you don't want me to do anything else? Make any other plans?"

"No. After dinner I thought maybe I would take you to Squaw Peak."

"To make out?" I joked, trying to fish out his true motive. He wouldn't propose on Squaw Peak, would he? Wait a minute. Why was I giving any credence to Rhonda's hunch that he was going to propose? I didn't think he was going to, so why was I listening to her?

"No, to see the view. I hear it's beautiful." He winked.

Usually it was the other way around. Most guys said they were going to Squaw Peak to see the view when they really wanted to make out. I raised an eyebrow. "Meaning you've never actually looked at the view when you were up there?"

"What kind of guy do you take me for?" Luke asked with feigned shock.

Knowing him, I decided he really did want to see the view. He was very sweet. "The kind of guy I'd go there with," I replied. I'd go with him almost anywhere. My favorite thing about him was it felt right to be with him. I didn't even need to fill in the silence. When I first met him, I would ramble on nervously, but since I'd gotten to know him, time with him was just comfortable. I could sit with him and not talk at all. Just like how he could say my name and nothing else and I felt it conveyed a thousand other things.

* * *

Having Luke planning the whole evening made me anxious. Were we going to a romantic restaurant or a casual restaurant or our ever-reliable Subway? I didn't know what to expect. Which led me back not only to my original problem of not knowing what to get him for a gift but also to my worry that there could be some added significance to the evening.

As I was getting ready for the date, Rhonda tried to convince me she was right, that Luke was going to propose. I kept denying it, mostly for her sake but maybe a little for my sake too. I finally banished her from my vicinity because she was freaking me out with all her excited theories. I was glad Sarah and Ashlee weren't around to add to the fervor.

I spent way too long deciding what to wear. Should I dress up? Dress down? Just be casual? Rhonda returned from exile to help me come up with the perfect outfit for the evening, but she wasn't helpful. She was so convinced Luke was going to propose that her opinion about what was appropriate to wear for this occasion pretty much didn't count. There was also the small issue of fashion sense. Let's just say I thought of Kate Middleton as a fashionista, and Rhonda knew her only as a princess.

Finally I called him. "Any suggestions for what I should wear?" I hoped I came off sounding casual and not like the knotted ball of nerves I was.

"I don't know. Something nice?"

That wasn't exactly helpful either.

I fished for clues. "Are we going to be outdoors?" I sure hoped not. I was allergic to outdoor activities. I always got injured. "Or indoors? Should I dress casual or . . . ?" I wanted him to fill in the blank.

"You always look nice, Soph. Just wear what you usually wear."

I hadn't always looked nice. My wardrobe had drastically changed since I'd known Luke. When we first met, I wore mainly sweats or pajamas. Target had a nice line of sleepwear that could almost pass as casual wear. *Very* casual wear. But as our relationship progressed and I gained more distance from my divorce, my apparel became much nicer. Meaning I got dressed now. No more frump clothes.

"No hints for where we're going?" I persisted.

He sounded like he was smiling. "That, Sophia, would ruin the surprise."

That didn't help matters.

"All right, then. I will go back to studying my closet, since you won't spill the secret." I was hoping to guilt him into telling me.

"It'll be worth the wait, Sophia."

Again, not helping. Rhonda would already have a ring on my finger from this conversation.

"Okay, well, see you soon. I hope I'm dressed okay for the occasion." It was my last-ditch effort.

I could hear the amusement in Luke's voice. "You'll look beautiful."

I hung up, frustrated that I couldn't get Luke to tell me any more about the night's activities. But I was running out of time to get ready, so I went with skinny jeans and a striped, fitted tee with a belted white sweater. Kate Middleton would approve.

When Luke picked me up, he was wearing jeans and a button-down shirt. Surely not the clothes one wears when proposing to his girlfriend, right? He didn't look dressed for a special occasion.

As he walked in the door, a thrill washed over me. I was glad he was my boyfriend.

After getting everything I needed, we went out to the car and headed north. I played a guessing game in my head about where we were going. The Provo Temple was north. Salt Lake was also north.

"What are you thinking?" Luke asked.

"I'm trying to figure out where we're going." Not the Provo Temple, since he'd just driven by it.

"It's a surprise," Luke reminded me. "But if you really need to know, I'll ruin it for you."

He turned off toward Provo Canyon. I crossed Salt Lake off my mental list.

I analyzed recent conversations and our relationship in general yet again. Was Luke really going to propose tonight? I still didn't think so. At least that was my gut feeling. What I had said to Rhonda was true: I really didn't think our relationship was at that point yet. We hadn't even said we loved each other yet. Honestly, I was afraid to get to that point.

I reviewed the timeline since we had started dating at the beginning of February. It had only been two months since we had really been a couple. On the other hand, Travis and I had dated just over a month by the time we'd gotten engaged. Then six weeks later we'd been married. The place where Luke and I were right now after two months of dating, though I wasn't exactly clear where that was, compared to where Travis and I had been after barely knowing each other for two months was totally different. Counting the time I'd known Luke before we'd started dating, I had known him and been dating him longer than my total relationship with Travis—dating, courtship, and marriage included. There was a vast time-spent-together difference.

Luke took me to eat at the same restaurant in Park City we'd gone to in February, the night of the big roommate group date. That was the night when my secret about being divorced was revealed in a big way when Claire showed up engaged to Travis. But this time I was not crashing from an adrenaline rush. This time I was more preoccupied with my thoughts than with maintaining the conversation.

"Hey." He tried to catch my eye. "I'm the one getting a year older. I'm one year away from being considered a menace to society. Why are you so quiet tonight?"

I figured I might as well tell the truth, get it all out in the open. "Rhonda thinks you're going to propose to me tonight."

"Oh." He paused. "Would you be disappointed if I didn't?"

"I think *she's* going to be disappointed. She's hoping for vicarious pleasure."

"But would *you*?" Luke persisted.

"Honestly, Luke, thinking about marriage scares me."

"Okay." The look on his face was a cross between perplexed and apprehensive. Was he worried about what I was going to say next?

I cleared my throat. "But that doesn't mean someday I won't feel differently. For now, please know I love being with you."

Luke still looked like he was waiting for me to say more. "But?"

"No buts. That's it," I reassured him.

"So I should keep the ring in my pocket?"

I stared at him. I literally felt all the blood drain from my face and my stomach tighten.

"Sophia," he laughed, "don't look so shocked. I'm just kidding."

Even though he said it was a joke, I was still having a hard time breathing.

He took my hand. "I realize it's a sensitive subject, and we don't have to rush into anything. I'm happy being with you too."

I took a deep breath, glad he let me off the hook. "Thank you. And," I continued lightly, "since it's your birthday, I should be the one surprising you."

A curious look crossed Luke's face. "Okay, what do you have in mind?"

"I have a gift for you. Do you want it?"

"Absolutely."

I hesitated momentarily as I handed him a wrapped package. I still wasn't sure if my gift was too personal, not personal enough, or just right. I had printed a picture book: *The Top Ten Times Spent with You.*

10. Turkeys
9. Subway
8. Confessions of sliding down a hill
7. Spilling slushies
6. Spending time "washing" laundry and eating Oreos with you
5. Introducing you to my family
4. PDA on your couch
3. Spilling bleach
2. Riding the ski lift in Park City
1. Right now

Accompanying the pages were pictures of each place with me posed in reenactment. Sarah had helped me by taking the pictures, and we had a good time making the book. It was one of the few times I had seen her smile in the last couple weeks.

I watched as he unwrapped it and turned the pages.

"I didn't know what to get you," I shyly explained, feeling stupid that I couldn't come up with any other ideas.

He examined the pictures. "It's great, Soph. We have good memories, don't we?"

His words caught me by surprise. Somehow, through all the hard times, he still thought of our times together as good memories. When I thought about it, many of my good times were the times spent with Luke. Even if I felt bad alone, I usually felt good being around him.

"Thanks," I blurted out, voicing what I thought needed to be said.

Despite the darkness, I could see how confused he looked. "For what?" he asked.

"Everything," I said simply, but in reality, *everything* did not even begin to cover it.

"I'm lucky I have you." He pulled me closer to him so he could kiss me.

"I'm the lucky one," I argued, really meaning it.

Luke scoffed. "Why do you think that?"

How to explain my feelings without sounding too heavy? "I'm glad I'm no longer where I was when I met you, and I don't want to screw up what we have."

"You're not screwing anything up. How could you?"

"Because I'm once bitten, twice shy. I'm not ready to talk about—"

"Sophia, if you're referring to what Rhonda said, don't let it bother you. I'm satisfied knowing you're my girl. We don't have to talk about that yet."

"It's not that it bothers me; it's that—"

"Sophia, shh; you don't need to say anything more." He put his hand in my hair and gently kissed me.

The waitress arriving with our food was a welcome diversion for me. Luke didn't bring the topic of our relationship back up, and I saw no reason to either. I tried to keep the focus of the conversation on how good the food was.

The drive back to Provo was a quiet one. I didn't know if it was just me, but the air felt heavy between us after all the talk of Rhonda's proposal suspicions.

I finally broke the silence. "What would be your ideal way to spend your birthday?"

He looked over at me. "Exactly how I spent it tonight: with you."

"No, I mean if I was trying to plan something, what would you like?"

"Other than spending time with you?"

"Yes. Say that's a given." I smiled.

"Okay. Let me think . . . I like to be with the people I love."

I wasn't going to touch that one. I was quiet again, watching the dark road as he drove us to Squaw Peak and parked.

He shut the truck off and turned to me. "How about you, Soph? When's your birthday, again?"

"August seventh."

"So we won't be at school together."

"Right." He was assuming we would still be together then. I liked that.

"And we wouldn't necessarily be celebrating it in Provo."

I was curious. "Does that play a big factor?"

"No, just thinking about my options. What would be the best way to spend your birthday?"

"Other than spending it with you?" I grinned, using his reasoning on himself.

He pretended to be serious. "Yes. I'm a given."

"Good food. Good company. Really good cake."

"Vegas or California?"

I shook my head. "I'm not sure."

"What about the Strip? Would you want to eat there or go see a show?"

"Depends on what the show is."

"Naturally."

"Are we talking *Thunder From Down Under?*" I said as seriously as I could manage.

"I thought you'd already seen that, being a native and all," he quipped back.

"My roommates might think so, but I never have." I started laughing.

Luke smiled and grabbed my hand. "Good. Let's keep it that way. Gyrating men in loincloths should be avoided at all costs."

"Definitely."

"I guess the Strip is out?" He pretended he was disappointed.

"At least that show." I giggled.

He thought for a moment. "Barbeque? Pool party?"

"How did this turn to being about me? I was trying to think of what could have made this night any better."

Luke shook his head. "Nothing. It was perfect."

Then he did what most people did on Squaw Peak: he kissed me.

Chapter Four

Road Trip to Vegas. Oh, Goody

A ROAD TRIP TO VEGAS. Oh, goody.

With finals behind us, it was our one last hurrah before we all went our separate ways for the summer. To most people, it would sound like the perfect way to celebrate the end of the semester, a guaranteed good time. To me . . . it sounded like a recipe for disaster or maybe just the potential for disaster, mostly because of the ingredients making up the recipe.

It all started when Dan invited Rhonda down to Vegas to see *Star Wars in Concert*. Rhonda, not having a car, did not ask Sarah, the only roommate with a car, for a ride. Asking Sarah was sketchy since she was still recovering from her broken engagement. Instead Rhonda turned to me. Not because I was her date's sister but because my boyfriend had a vehicle and might be willing to drive. So what should have just involved Rhonda exponentially multiplied into me going, Luke driving, Justin joining, and Ashlee tagging along. Chances were, with Rhonda and Ashlee in the same vehicle on the same road trip, there'd at least be some good treats.

We invited Sarah, but as expected, she opted out, claiming she had things to do. I was pretty sure I knew what kind of "things" she'd be doing. I used to do those kinds of "things." Things like crying and reviewing my relationship to try to figure out where it went wrong. But Sarah's not going worked out in the end, since there wasn't enough room for both Sarah *and* Ashlee. Then Sarah decided to go back home for the summer, so ultimately everyone was accounted for.

The plan was to leave on Friday afternoon and stay Saturday, and then Dan would drive Rhonda and Ashlee back to Provo after church on Sunday, and Luke and Justin would head to California.

It seemed, from the outside, like a simple weekend trip in which all of Rhonda's hopes and dreams for her date would be fulfilled. I had a feeling it could quickly become something so much more than that.

I unearthed my duffel bag from the depths of my closet, which should have been easy since almost everything was packed, but the things I didn't want to deal with, like the laundry I never folded and the papers I hadn't sorted, somehow managed to pile up back there. As I started packing the last of what I wanted to keep from my closet, I found the letter I had received from my former roommate Gretchen Clark, who was currently on a mission in New Zealand. It was folded into a tiny rectangle and buried under some jeans.

I also found my wedding ring in one of the zippered end-pouches of the duffle bag. I had sort of forgotten about it. I had put it there back in January and hadn't thought any more about it until now. I opened the velvet box and looked at the one-carat, heart-shaped diamond ring; seeing it again didn't make me miss Travis any. In fact, I didn't feel anything looking at that ring. And that felt good.

I put it back in the bag. I didn't know what to do with it and didn't want to think about it, and that was most easily accomplished by bringing it home.

Then there was Gretchen's letter. I felt like the worst friend ever, seemingly dropping off the radar for her whole mission. When Travis left me, I stopped checking my e-mail and made no effort to keep in touch with anyone, including her. I reread the letter, then decided to send off a quick e-mail now so I wouldn't forget later. I sent it to the address listed at the top of the page, hoping it was still current.

Dear Gretchen,

Please don't hate me. So much has happened since you've been gone. You know how everyone says a mission can change your life? Well, I've kind of had that happen to me. My life has completely changed since you left.

Travis and I are divorced. He left me last April with not much of an explanation or warning. I was completely devastated. I went back home to my parents and stayed there through the summer. It was so heartbreaking and shocking, I kept waiting to wake up from the bad dream. I kept hoping he'd want me back. Needless to say, I was very depressed.

I went back to BYU in the fall (under much protest). Things didn't really get any more normal. It was pretty crazy. I wish you had been my roommate at that point; maybe then it wouldn't have been so hard. But long story short, I'm doing much better, and we have so much to talk about. Travis ended up marrying one of my ROOMMATES. My brother, Dan, is dating another one of my roommates. And I think you need to be my roommate when you get back. I need some normalcy with my roommate situation. But the best news out of all of this mess is that I met Luke, and we just started dating, and he's pretty incredible. You'll have to meet him when you get home. I'm going back to Vegas for the summer. Call me when you get home. Obviously I have so much to catch you up on.

I hope the mission has gone well. I'm sorry I've been a terrible friend. But I can't wait to see you soon and hear about your mission and all.

Love,

Sophia

Luke came over as I was finishing packing. He picked up the bag to carry it to the truck, but because it was still unzipped, he saw the jewelry box. He set the bag down. "What's this?" he asked, pulling it out.

"It's, uh, my . . ." I tried to sound casual. Even though the ring no longer meant anything, it still was an uncomfortable situation to be in with Luke. "It's my wedding ring from Travis."

There was an ever-so-slight pause. "And you still have it?" he said.

I nodded. "I kind of lost track of it."

"But you still have it?" he repeated. He was irritated.

"I haven't decided what to do with it yet."

"What's to decide?" Luke's expression was hard.

"I'm not keeping it for sentimental reasons. I just haven't gotten rid of it yet."

"That clears it up," Luke said in a flat voice.

"It's not that big a deal," I said, hoping to diffuse the building tension.

"It's not?" Luke raised an eyebrow. "It makes me feel like you haven't moved on."

Ouch. "It's not like I still wear it. I had it when I came to school last year, that's all. Things have changed since then."

"Have they?" Luke looked straight at me.

I took his hand. "Luke. Travis means nothing. The ring means nothing. After I confronted Travis, I threw it in my bag, and I seriously forgot about it until I got my bag out to pack for this trip. I should sell it. I have no reason to keep it."

"You sure about that, Soph?"

"I am sure about that." I felt like I was reassuring not only him but myself as well. I was glad it didn't turn into a full-blown fight about Travis. Somehow I had to keep his presence from lurking in my relationship with Luke, and only I could do that.

He stood there for a minute, turning the box in his hand slowly. "Can I look?"

"Sure."

He opened the velvet box. "So this is the ring?"

I nodded. "That was the ring."

"Did he choose it, or did you?"

"He did."

"Were you okay with that?"

"At the time I was. I just wanted to marry him."

Luke looked over at me. "And now?"

I shrugged. "It wouldn't have been my first choice in cut. It has less sentimental value than if it had been a ring I'd fallen in love with."

"So you didn't like your ring?"

"I did at the time. I thought it was romantic that he'd chosen a heart-shaped diamond. Now it has no meaning to me whatsoever."

"You sure?" Luke still wanted reassurance.

"It doesn't mean anything," I reconfirmed. There was a moment of silence. "We should probably get going; everyone will be waiting." I stood and took his hand.

"Let the road trip begin." Luke gave a pained expression, and we headed out to join the others.

* * *

Rhonda had been counting down the days to the upcoming weekend and was so excited she was practically jumping out of her skin. She and Ashlee endlessly discussed plans and possibilities for that weekend. Then they would giggle. I wondered how the Ashlee factor would play into the weekend equation.

I'd never spent much time with Ashlee. Even living with her for the last month, I didn't see her much because I was usually with Luke. In fact, I was guilty of trying to avoid her at times. She was a nice enough girl, but way too, I don't know, *enthusiastic* for me. Or maybe it was more that she was too enthusiastic about things I was not enthusiastic about, so we didn't have a lot to enthuse about together—unlike Rhonda, who was just like Ashlee and absolutely loved the same exact things. And that was why they were BFFs.

When Ashlee first moved in, she was infatuated with Luke, so when things with Luke and me started to get serious, it made it a little awkward to have Ashlee swooning over him. After she found out he and I were a couple, she turned her affections to Justin. Now he had the privilege of sitting next to her the whole trip. We weren't even out of Provo before she started with what she called "road trip games."

"Okay, guys, so I was thinking, since we have a long drive, we should play some games."

It reminded me of the first time we had FHE last semester and we played get-to-know-you games. Were we really going to have to suffer through six hours of "games"? Please. Tell. Me. No.

She continued. "We could start with twenty questions to get to know each other better."

Who did we need to get to know better? We'd been together the whole semester. I was afraid of questions that helped others get to know me better. Besides, I was already getting to know Luke, and Rhonda and Ashlee already knew each other well, so it might turn into a "bombard Justin with the whole twenty questions" session. Or me. And I didn't want to answer twenty questions about my divorce.

"That's so fun." Rhonda was delighted with the idea. Then she did her little clapping-in-succession thingy. Yes, this was going to be a long six hours.

Ashlee began. "Since it's my idea, I'll ask the questions first. We can all go around and give answers. Okay?"

Ashlee fired away at the questions like one would on a first date, but she expected each and every person to answer. No one was allowed to pass on any question.

"What's the worst thing you've ever done to someone you were in a romantic relationship with?" she asked.

I felt all these questions would somehow be indirectly directed at me, as if Ashlee was trying to ask somewhat vague questions to find out about my marriage.

"I broke up with a girl I was dating in high school two weeks before Christmas so I didn't have to buy her a present," Justin admitted.

"No." Ashlee's eyes opened wide.

"Justin," Rhonda chastised him. "That's pretty immature."

"I was in *high school*. That makes it excusable."

I had too many "worsts" to count involving not only Travis but his family too: accidentally giving my ex-in-laws food poisoning at Thanksgiving, inducing an allergic reaction on purpose to get out of lunch with my mother-in-law, returning all the furniture Travis and I bought on the credit card without telling him first . . . "I'll pass," I said.

"Nope, that's not allowed. Game rules," Justin said teasingly. I think he was just as curious about my divorce as Rhonda and Ashlee, but he was more tactful about inquiring.

"Okay." I took a breath before choosing from my "worst things" list. I took the liberty of adjusting my answer a little and applying it to the lunch date with my mother-in-law. "I ate shrimp on purpose even though I'm allergic to it to end a lunch date."

"You did not," Rhonda said.

"It wasn't going very well, and I didn't think my allergic reaction would be as bad as it was." I felt sheepish admitting it.

"Sounds like you were desperate," Rhonda said. "What about you, Luke?" she asked, moving on.

"I can't think of anything. Probably the worst thing I've ever done on a date, though, was on a double date with Justin when I agreed to pretend with him that he was from Australia."

"Australia?" Ashlee looked over at Justin.

Justin shrugged. "Girls like foreign accents."

"And what about you, Ashlee?" Rhonda prompted her.

She tipped her head. "I ignored the guy I went to homecoming with because I really wanted to go to the dance, just not with him."

No one commented.

"C'mon, guys. We're talking high school, remember?" she said to justify her answer like Justin had. She continued with the game. "What's the most embarrassing thing you've ever done?"

Justin snorted to himself.

Rhonda picked up on it immediately. "What? You obviously have something good to tell."

"Every Christmas my dad made our whole family dress up as Santa and his elves and go Christmas caroling to the families in the ward. I'm talking not once but twice, sometimes three Sundays, in the month of

December. He was all gung ho about it, and we had costumes, including tights and everything. It was so embarrassing, especially when I was a teenager and we visited families with girls my age."

I laughed until I got a side cramp. "Justin, obviously it helped you develop a great sense of humor. Not just anybody could pull that off."

He rolled his eyes. "At the time, it was awful."

"Everything in high school is awful," I said.

"Rhonda?" Ashlee looked at her.

"One time at church the young women were singing in sacrament meeting. I forgot the piano was playing an extra introductory part, and I started singing all by myself. It was really embarrassing."

I shared how I'd spilled a slushie all over Luke.

Luke grimaced. "The first BYU football game I ever went to, my roommate convinced me to paint a big blue *Y* down the middle of my face. But I got a sunburn at the game, and I had to walk around with those tan lines for a long time."

We all looked at Ashlee.

"I walked into church with my skirt tucked into my nylons," Ashlee said before asking the next question without hesitation. "How have you changed since high school?"

Wasn't it time for someone else to start asking the questions?

Justin said he dated more now than in high school. Luke grew twelve inches and put on forty pounds. Ashlee volunteered that she didn't go to so many parties now, and Rhonda said she was a better cook. Me? I was a completely different person than I had been in high school. That had been only two years ago, but my whole life had changed. And with everything I had been through since then, high school felt like two lifetimes ago. Instead of sharing that, I went with something different. "I had braces forever."

As I expected, Ashlee shifted the conversation back to relationships and dating. "So do you guys believe in love at first sight?"

Justin answered first. "My vote is still for that wolf imprinting idea. You see the person and just know. Love at first sight, instant attraction."

Ashlee hadn't been around the last time Justin explained his theories on love. If she had been, she would have realized Justin wasn't into her, since he was leaning toward the "knowing immediately" factor when it came to dating girls. I hoped she was digesting what he was saying because there was no imprinting happening in the backseat, at least not on Justin's part.

"Instant attraction is easy," I scoffed at Justin. "It happens all over campus every day."

"I'm not talking about just physical attraction. It's like when you talk to them and you know."

I laughed out loud. "Who knew you were such a romantic, Justin? You've been watching too many of Rhonda's Disney movies."

"I think it's possible," Rhonda backed up Justin.

Did that mean she thought she and my brother were already in love? And if so, what did that mean for me? "Was it love at first sight with Dan?" I asked her. I was curious now.

"Well, no, not love, but I was instantly attracted to him."

It wasn't hard for Rhonda to be instantly attracted to any guy. She had a thing for testosterone.

"What about you?" Ashlee looked at me. "You're the most experienced, relationship-wise. Was it like that for you?"

I stiffened. I didn't mind talking to Luke about Travis, but only in private. "If you mean most experienced because I was married, I've got to disagree. That was part of the problem. I was inexperienced and fell for the first guy who came along." I hoped Luke didn't think I fell for him just because he was the second guy who had come along. "As for Travis, his track record seems to support that he believes in love at first sight."

"Well, Sophia, I'm still having a hard time getting over the idea that you were married before," Ashlee said. "What's the story behind that whole thing?"

"I'm still not at a point where I want to talk about it. Someday," I said gently. I mean, I felt like I was over Travis, but then he went and got remarried, and it upset me that he moved on so quickly. It was weird. I felt like every time I had a little bit of normalcy back, he did something to upset my tranquility. We weren't even married anymore, and he still had a way of affecting my life.

"But Luke knows about it."

"That's because he's my boyfriend, Ashlee." It still gave me a thrill calling Luke my boyfriend.

"But you told him pretty quick. He knew about it on the group date."

Actually, he had known for months, even before we'd started dating. "Luke and I had been together for two weeks before the group date."

Ashlee paused, a surprised and puzzled look on her face. "What?"

Rhonda joined in immediately. "Yeah. What?"

"Did you know about this?" Ashlee turned to Justin.

A satisfied look crept across his face. "I had my suspicions."

"You guys were already dating?" Rhonda asked.

"Yup." I knew my admission was going to bring more questions. Maybe it was time to answer some of them.

"Really?" I pictured Rhonda reviewing all the times Luke and I had been together and how she had missed that something was going on.

"I have one word for you," Justin joined in. "Laundry room." He thought for a moment. "Wait, maybe that's two?"

"The laundry room? That's what was going on? The night you spilled the bleach?" Ashlee turned to Rhonda. "See? I knew she was acting strange."

Luke suppressed a smile but said nothing. Yeah, there was a little more than laundry going on that night. That was the first time Luke kissed me. He rested his hand on my knee and squeezed gently. He didn't have to say anything; the small act of affection conveyed his feelings.

Rhonda's eyes narrowed. "Are there any other huge secrets you're keeping from us?"

"My thoughts exactly," Justin jumped in.

"Nope. I think divorced and dating Luke on the down low about covers it." I decided to completely change the subject. "What are your plans this summer, Ashlee? Are you going home at all?"

"Nope. I don't get a lot of time off. Besides, my dad is still mad about my going to hair school and coming to Provo."

"He doesn't like Provo?" Justin asked the same question I was going to ask.

"He doesn't like hair school. He wanted me to go to regular college."

"Huh," I said.

"But hair is Ashlee's calling in life, and she has to follow that," Rhonda piped up.

"What are you doing this summer, Justin?" Ashlee asked.

"Alaskan fisheries. Working to make the big bucks."

"Sounds stinky." Ashlee wrinkled her nose, then paused a beat. "Has anyone heard from Claire since the shower? Are they on their honey—" Ashlee glanced at me and stopped midsentence. I must have been scowling without realizing it.

I'm not sure who in our group would have heard anything other than herself or Rhonda. "I'm not exactly friends with Claire," I said. "Or Travis, for that matter."

Justin chuckled. "Claire is definitely not my type."

"What is your type?" Ashlee pounced on the opening in the conversation.

Justin blew out a breath. "Not Claire."

I think Ashlee decided to drop the conversation. Justin didn't seem like he was going to expound.

Three hours into the road trip and Ashlee had yet to stop chattering. She had managed to provide a running and sometimes amusing commentary the whole time, but I could tell by the expression on Justin's face that he was tired of her. It was about that point that Ashlee started double popping her gum. "There's really nothing out here, is there?" She looked out the windows.

Midsentence Justin put in his earphones.

Then there was the lotion Ashlee kept putting on. The smell continually wafted up to the front seat. I was about to ask what it was when Justin beat me to it.

"What is that smell?" He crinkled his nose.

"Lotion," Ashlee replied, implying *obviously*.

"You smell like a fruit basket." Justin apparently wasn't a fan. It *was* a little strong.

"I'm getting car sick," Ashlee suddenly announced.

"Maybe it's that lotion," Justin suggested.

"I'll stop and get some Dramamine," Luke said, and not waiting for Ashlee to answer, he pulled off at the next exit and stopped at the first gas station.

Everyone piled out, happy to stretch our legs and probably secretly relieved to have a break from Ashlee's antics.

"So, if you order shrimp while we're on a date, I'll know things aren't going well," Luke said as we walked together to the store.

"It's a long story," I admitted. "Not something I'm proud of."

"I'm still curious." He was grinning.

"I was out to lunch with my mother-in-law. Travis and I had only been married a couple of weeks, and I still wanted her to like me. While we were eating, she handed me a credit card bill for almost nine thousand dollars."

"Wow. Was it all your charges?"

"Yeah. Travis and I put our honeymoon on it and bought furniture. I was under the mistaken impression his parents were paying for it all. Travis kept saying, 'My mom said make sure we get this and make sure we get that.'"

"That's a pretty steep bill."

"Especially when I was supporting us with two minimum-wage jobs. I was a bit dumbfounded when I saw how much the bill was. Maxine had this satisfied smile on her face, almost like she was enjoying how shocked I was."

"That was it? She just gave it to you?"

"She said, 'I believe this is yours.' I think I managed something like, 'Travis didn't tell me how much this would be.' Maxine patted my hand and said, 'Communication is important in marriage.'"

"I probably would have eaten shrimp too."

"But that's not the worst of it, Luke," I said quietly.

His eyebrows shot up. "There's more?"

"Not one of my finer moments. I had all the furniture repossessed from where we bought it. And I didn't tell Travis until after I did it."

"Really? Why?"

"Like I said, we weren't making very much money. Every time I tried talking to Travis about our finances, he brushed me off. Then Travis and I had a fight, and I got sick of him being concerned about only what he wanted, so I made the executive decision that the furniture had to go. Besides, I figured if I returned all the furniture, we could erase most of our debt."

"Drastic," Luke said.

"It probably added to the demise of my marriage, but I was so stressed out I wasn't thinking clearly, and"—I paused—"it was almost like we were pretending to be adults but without the responsibility. Travis didn't want to deal with the reality that we wouldn't get out of debt for years, and I thought returning the furniture was the most responsible thing to do."

"Travis got pretty mad that you decided this yourself?"

"I'd suggested it before, but he was against it. He thought it wasn't a big deal that we were in debt, and he thought we deserved to have nice stuff. Like I said, I kind of made a rash decision."

"I don't think it was a bad thing to want to not be in debt." Luke squeezed my hand.

"So do you think I'm a crazy psycho woman now?"

"Nah, I would never think that."

"But if you start offering me Dramamine, I should be suspicious?"

"Yeah," Luke said, smiling.

We went into the store and picked up some snacks and drinks and the all-important Dramamine. Within twenty minutes of being back on the road and having Dramamine pumping through her system, chatty Ashlee was asleep.

"Now, this is the best part of the trip," Justin said, settling himself down as if he was going to take a nap too.

Ashlee's head kept bobbing onto his shoulder. It was too bad she was asleep and missing the whole thing. She would have been so excited to know she was touching him. Justin kept trying to put her head back where it belonged, but it never stayed. She slept the rest of the way to Vegas, and I realized Dramamine was the best-kept secret ever.

Chapter Five
Gretchen's Gauge

DAN AND RHONDA DISAPPEARED THE moment we arrived in Vegas, so I assumed the roles of entertainer and tour guide for the rest of the group. And my question about what would happen with Ashlee once we got here was quickly answered. She was my responsibility this trip. Since she and Justin weren't a couple, it turned into a third-wheel deal, and no one benefited. Luke and I were comfortable enough in our relationship that adding Justin to our plans didn't feel like we had a third wheel. But we couldn't just leave Ashlee home with my parents, so I fell into the hostess position and created a sort of unofficial double date.

On Saturday we did the biggest touristy thing and went down to the Strip. I usually tried to avoid it, but Ashlee had never been to Vegas and begged to go everywhere we could on the Strip until I submitted. We rode the roller coaster at New York New York (Justin had to sit with Ashlee since that was how the numbers paired us off), saw the fountains at the Bellagio, and went to the top of the Stratosphere. We—mostly she—took pictures. She bought souvenirs. By the time we hit a buffet, I was ready to sit down for a while. Our sightseeing had been quite a feat for any tourist on any day. But then Ashlee also wanted to see the temple.

We were already halfway there location-wise, but I was exhausted. Unfortunately she returned to her suggesting and resuggesting the idea until we finally gave in, sort of like a child begging and bugging her parents until they gave in. We went to see the temple.

Back when I was dating Travis, if we had gone to the temple, I would have for sure assumed he was going to ask me to marry him. Was there any other point in visiting it? But my mind frame had drastically changed, and

I didn't think a thing about going there with Luke. Besides, this was more of a sightseeing thing than a romantic thing.

"Is this where you got married?" Ashlee asked as we walked around the grounds.

"No, Salt Lake."

She stopped, confused. "Salt Lake? Why? You're from here."

"That's where Travis was from and what he wanted. At the time it seemed like a good idea." At the time I mostly cared about marrying him. He convinced me that *where* didn't matter. He must have convinced Claire of that too because the Las Vegas Strip was a long way away from the Salt Lake Temple.

"When you got married—?"

"Ashlee, I'm with Luke now. I don't want to talk about Travis," I whispered nicely.

"Oh," she said, looking wounded.

"Travis is a jerk. He gets what he deserves by running off with Claire."

"That's kind of harsh," Ashlee said.

I sighed. "What he did to me was kind of harsh too."

When we returned home dead tired, I walked into the kitchen to find a scary scene that made me stop. My mom, Dan, and Rhonda were in the kitchen, all wearing cute, frilly aprons (yes, including Dan), making pastel-colored Rice Krispy treats.

"Oh, you're back." My mom looked up, positively beaming. Was it because she found in Rhonda the daughter she'd never had? "We're making treats for tomorrow." My mom clapped in succession. Oh, she and Rhonda were a scary combination. The fact that they'd been able to get Dan into the kitchen and wearing an apron was horrifying. He had something more than a bad case of spring fever if he was willing to wear an apron for a girl, probably more along the lines of a bad case of love.

"Would you guys like to help?" my mom asked. "Only if I get to wear an apron," Justin said.

His comment caught my mom off guard, causing her to stop and look at him curiously for a moment.

"I want to help too." Ashlee immediately walked over and rolled up her sleeves. I wasn't sure if it had to do with baking or Justin volunteering.

Didn't they just spend the entire day with us, walking the same Strip, visiting the same casinos, driving to the same temple? Shouldn't they have been just as tired as Luke and me?

Luke, Justin, and I sat down at the island opposite where they were working, and my mom went into the pantry.

"How was *Star Wars in Concert*?" I asked.

"It was amazing," Rhonda said.

Justin leaned over to Dan. "How did you get roped into that?" he asked in a hushed voice.

Dan looked surprised. "I asked her."

Rhonda was still talking, filling in all the details for Ashlee, oblivious to the other conversation going on.

I could tell Justin felt like he had just put his foot in his mouth. "The apron too, though, dude?"

"Oh, is that what you meant?"

Justin was probably talking about the date with Rhonda, but he went along with Dan. "Yeah."

My mother walked back into the kitchen and over to Justin. "Here you go," she said, handing him yet another flowery, frilly apron.

Justin grinned as he put it on. "All *right*."

"And you." She gave Ashlee one as well. Just how many of those aprons did my mom have, and why?

I took a picture of Justin with my phone, solely for the purpose of blackmail. "We're going upstairs," I announced, dismissing Luke and me.

"Make sure you leave your door open," my mom called after us.

My cheeks burned. "I'm not going to fornicate," I muttered.

"That was not what I was suggesting," she said in a firm voice.

I backpedaled. "Well, then, I was completely joking." I tried to laugh, but it sounded more like a cough.

Luke followed me silently up the stairs. At the top, I turned to him, but before I could say anything, he held up both hands. "Don't worry. I promise I'll behave."

I grabbed his hand and led him into my room, breathing a sigh of relief. Finally Luke and I were alone, leaving everyone downstairs happily making treats like they were children instead of adults.

"So this is your room?" Luke looked around, and I suddenly felt self-conscious. Having him in my room made me feel exposed for some reason, though I had no idea why. He had seen me crying. He had been there right after I'd confronted Travis. He'd been with me the night of the Big Date when Travis and Claire showed up engaged. What *hadn't* Luke witnessed in my life, other than my state of being immediately after my divorce? He knew me better than anyone, so why was I suddenly shy to have him in my room? Or maybe it was my mother's warning.

He sat on the edge of my bed, and I chose the chair at my desk.

"There's too much homemaking going on downstairs." I opened my eyes wide like I was scared.

A smile crossed Luke's lips. "Yeah. What's that all about?"

"I think it's called synergy. Whatever it is, it worries me. My mom and Rhonda are too much alike, and Dan seems a little too gaga over her."

"Do you see something happening with them?"

I nodded my head emphatically. "Oh, yes. Between Rhonda and my mom playing Holly Homemaker down there and Dan happily joining in, they're way past the marriage material stage. They may even be heading into the next stage."

"The marriage material stage? The next stage? What are you talking about?"

"My roommate from freshman year, Gretchen, had a gauge to measure guys we dated: S.S. for sweet spirit, meaning the guy did nothing for me; M.M. for marriage material, the guy had potential; and E.C. for eternal companion, I could totally marry the guy."

"So what would I be?"

I shouldn't have been stupid enough to put myself in that position. Of course he was going to ask. Who wouldn't wonder? But, then, I was in the sticky situation where I felt way more than I was ready to admit, because it scared the heck out of me. I could feel the blush starting. "Are you going to make me say it?"

"Why not? I'm curious." His eyes stared at me intensely. He was looking very appealing at the moment.

I squirmed a little. "No." I shook my head. "It's embarrassing."

"C'mon, Soph. I want to know. You don't have to be embarrassed."

I tried to buy time. "Soon, okay; just not now." I wasn't sure if I had any intention of following through on that.

"Why not now?"

"Luke." I was bordering on slight panic. I hated talking about love and feelings. "I really want to be able to . . ." I really wanted to what? I wasn't sure. "It's not because of you. It's because of Travis."

His expression hardened. "Haven't we been through this? Aren't we done with Travis?"

I could feel my cheeks flush again. "You already know I am. It's just . . ."

"What?" he asked, waiting.

"I just need a little more time," I pleaded.

He looked at me, wary. "If you say so."

That moment in my bedroom could have been totally romantic. I could've said he was eternal companion material, and we would have moved forward, but I chickened out. Moving forward scared me almost more than anything, because we all know the rhyme, "First comes love, then comes . . ." and my wounds were still too fresh to take that leap of faith and admit I was falling in love with Luke. I leaned in to kiss him, hoping he wasn't too mad. He didn't say anything, and he pulled back instead of kissing me.

"I really am sorry I have so many hang ups. I think of Travis and what a jerk he is, and—"

"I hate talking about Travis, so how about we don't?"

"Sorry," I said, feeling slightly chastised. Not because of what Luke said but because I knew I shouldn't keep harping on the Travis topic. It never ended well. I tried to kiss Luke again and felt better when he finally hugged me and kissed me back.

If I hadn't been so busy kissing him, I probably would have heard my mom coming up the stairs. But I didn't hear her until she cleared her throat. Luke and I scooted apart so fast I lost my balance and slid off the side of the bed.

"Mom!" I managed, rubbing my backside.

"Sophia, I thought I made it clear—"

"I left the door open, Mom," I cut in, trying to gracefully climb back onto my bed. "We weren't doing anything."

Luke coughed and ran a hand through his hair. I glanced at him and could see pink crawling up his neck.

"Well, from what I saw, it sure looked like you were doing something."

"You're right, Sister Davis. I'm sorry," Luke said.

She looked over at Luke, then back at me. "Uh-huh. I was young once too. And then there's the real reason I came up here; dinner is ready." Mom gave us a knowing look before heading back down the hall.

"Well, that was uncomfortable," I whispered to Luke before I busted out laughing. "I can't believe my mom caught us kissing."

"I figured I better take the blame."

"Either way she'll hold it against me," I said, then imitated my mother. "'Sophia, remember that time I caught you making out on your bed with Luke?' This is not the last time I'll hear about it."

"Maybe she'll forget about it," Luke said.

"Not likely. But maybe she'll catch Dan and Rhonda making out, and then she'll have nothing to hold against me." I laughed. "I have a feeling Rhonda will be around a lot this summer."

My suspicions were confirmed as we walked into the kitchen. Rhonda stood right next to my mother, helping her get dinner together. Dan was setting the table, and Ashlee was placing frozen rolls on a cookie sheet to bake. I was surprised my mom and Rhonda weren't making homemade rolls. Maybe Rhonda thought this weekend had sealed the deal with her landing a husband and she didn't need to impress him by making homemade bread. Or maybe she didn't want to dazzle and/or blind him with all of her amazing domestic skills all at once.

Luke and I joined Justin and my dad at the dinner table, where they were reading different sections of the newspaper. I watched Rhonda and Ashlee burst out in random, spontaneous bouts of whispering, giggling, and clapping. One of the times they started giggling, Justin leaned over to me and whispered, "What is wrong with them?"

"That's how girls are when they've had a really good date and really like the guy they went out with," I whispered back.

"I've never seen you act that way." Justin playfully elbowed me.

"Ha ha, Justin."

Dinner was relatively quiet, with no more bouts of laughter from Rhonda and Ashlee. The long day finally caught up to everyone, and we were more interested in eating than talking.

My parents excused themselves after dinner, then we sat down to watch a movie, but most of us ended up dozing off. Dan and Rhonda were the ones who woke everyone up when the movie was over, and we all stumbled off to our designated sleeping places, relieved the day was finally over now.

Chapter Six
The Spring of My Discontent

WITH IMPENDING GOOD-BYES, THE next day was solemn, with the exception of Rhonda. She was positively giddy. She had been talking earlier to Ashlee, and from what I had heard, Rhonda sounded like she was floating on cloud nine. She was like Mount Vesuvius, spewing forth excitement about her date, analyzing every aspect of conversation, body language, and time spent together because that was what girls did. It was obvious she and Dan had hit it off very well. And as an added bonus, she had hit it off very well with her boyfriend's mother. Her future was looking bright.

Dan was driving Rhonda and Ashlee back up to Provo. They would have stayed longer, but Rhonda had landed her dream job working at the Disney store, and Ashlee still had hairdressing school. Luke and Justin had time commitments: Luke was going to Europe for spring term for a study abroad, and Justin had decided to head to Alaska.

Luke waited until Justin had loaded his stuff and climbed into the truck before pulling me in to say good-bye.

"Don't go off and find some European chick, okay?" I hoped to come off funny, but my voice sounded slightly strangled.

"I'm going there to check out old buildings, not girls." He wrapped me in a tight hug.

"Promise?" I whispered.

He tucked a strand of hair behind my ear. "Soph, you and I have an undeniable connection." He kissed me softly on the top of my head.

"Maybe you're right," I murmured, considering his words. When he said things like that, it was hard to feel insecure. Now, if only there wasn't going to be a continent and ocean between us.

"Oh, I know I'm right," Luke teased, then leaned in and kissed me again.

I didn't argue with that.

Justin opened the passenger door and poked his head up over the cab. "All right, you two, disentangle. We need to hit the road."

I stepped away from Luke. "You're just jealous," I said to Justin, using my favorite comeback.

"You're absolutely right," Justin said with a nod, "but I am heading off to the great state of Alaska, where I'll probably meet more women than I can handle."

"Whatever, Justin." Luke rolled his eyes.

"Hey, you never know." Justin defended his claim. He stood there for a few beats before getting back into the truck.

"I'm going to miss you," Luke said softly.

"I don't even want to think about it." I frowned.

"Maybe once I get back, you can come visit me?"

"I would love to," I said.

"Other than that, you're going to have to be happy with the online version of me."

"That might not be good enough," I swallowed, feeling my throat constricting.

"Wish it could be different, but it will be okay." He gave me another squeeze. Justin beeped the horn.

Luke ignored his impatience and instead took out his phone. "How about a quick picture?" We snapped a couple of pictures with Luke's phone. I was all for delaying the inevitable, but finally I had to let him go.

My parents came out to say good-bye to everyone. I hated that everyone was leaving. But like Luke said, it would be okay. Or at least I was going to work hard to convince myself. We waved them off, and I hurried into the house. I just needed a moment, or a day, and then I'd get over it.

I was teary-eyed when my mom caught up to me. She took one look at me, and I half expected her to break into the song "Tomorrow" from *Annie*. She didn't. "Chin up, honey, he'll be back before you know it" was what she said instead.

It didn't feel that way, but I put on a smile. I was going to use some old advice and fake it until I made it. I wanted to avoid any more words of advice. My mom was too practical for drama. So instead, I sniffed. "I know it."

She pulled me into a hug, something we normally didn't do. "Sophia, the way Luke looks at you says it all. He has my seal of approval."

I choked up and made my escape to my bedroom to have a quick sob in private. I was hoping if I indulged my emotions, maybe I could keep them in check for the rest of the day.

I was surprised to find my mom waiting for me when I came out. I needed some Visine from the bathroom because I knew my glassy red eyes were a dead giveaway to what I'd been doing in my bedroom. I stepped backward into my room, thinking if I retreated again, my mom might not notice I'd been crying.

"You know, Sophia . . ." Mom said as she followed me into my room and sat down on the edge of my bed.

Uh-oh. I was probably going to get a lecture. Or a pep talk. My mom was big on PMA, also known as positive mental attitude, and she often reminded me about the virtues of it because I struggled with it. It reminded me of how depressed Cali Hanson had been when I'd first met her and how my first impulse had been to try to do something to make it better so she wouldn't have to suffer. So I reminded myself to be patient and hear my mom out because she only wanted me to be happy.

"I know you're going to miss Luke, but I also know if you look for ways to help others instead of focusing on yourself the whole time, you will feel better, and time will pass more quickly. Make a goal to do one thing every day."

That might be stretching it for me. I wasn't sure I had the energy or motivation to be that dedicated to her idea. But my mom's words made sense. I nodded. "I can give it a try." It might be better than dwelling on Luke's absence.

Mom went off satisfied that the situation was rectified.

I focused my thoughts on ways to keep busy this summer. My deep thoughts didn't have time to become too deep, though, before my mom returned. "Hey, I forgot to tell you Cali wants you to call her. I think she needs you to babysit again."

"Okay, thanks," I said, happy for the diversion. I rolled over and sat up, thinking about Cali once again. I'd babysat for her for a couple of weeks during Christmas break. With all that had happened this semester, I hadn't kept in touch with her like I'd meant to. I usually got an update on her when I spoke with my mom. It would be nice to catch up, I thought as I found her name in my phone. "Cali? It's Sophia."

"Hey, how are you?" She sounded upbeat. "Are you coming back at all this summer?"

"Just got back."

"What are you doing?"

I didn't know if she meant today or the summer. "Right now? Missing my boyfriend."

"Your boyfriend?" Cali sounded intrigued. "Who is he? Is he that guy who visited at Christmas?"

My heart fluttered. "Yes, Luke. That would be him."

"So he did like you." I could hear her smiling.

"You could say that." I thought back to the memory from Christmas when I was still blind to Luke's feelings.

"Where is he from? Is he home for the summer?" I could hear the sympathy in her voice.

"He's from California but went to Europe. Study abroad. He comes back in six weeks."

As if I didn't have the time counted down to the days.

"Will you be here all summer?"

"Yes." Summer suddenly seemed long.

"Would you be interested in watching Joy? I'm not happy with her daycare situation, and if you could watch her the rest of the summer, it would give me time to find something better."

"Um, yeah, sure." That would give me something to do, and I'd earn some money and not have to go job hunting. "I might have plans to visit Luke when he gets back at the end of June though."

"Which might perfectly coincide with my vacation."

"Perfect."

"That helps me out so much, Sophia. Thank you."

"Actually, you're kind of doing me a favor. My mom wants to make sure I am doing something useful with my time. She would frown on my pining-for-my-boyfriend tendencies."

Cali laughed a little. "It'll be great to see you again."

"Boy, do I have stories to tell you. It has been a wild ride at school since I last saw you."

"Really?"

"My roommate and ex-husband got married."

I heard an intake of breath. "Oh, honey. Your ex-husband and your roommate? That's sort of a slap in the face."

"Yeah, pretty much," I agreed.

"Are you okay?"

"Aw, I'll be fine. It's just one of those things. I figure he'll get what he deserves, so . . ." I trailed off, then finished. "Anyway, there's so much more to tell you."

"Oh, good. All I talk about is diapers, sleeping schedules, and work."

I laughed. "This is way better."

"We'll have to catch up, then."

"See you soon."

"Take care."

My phone rang immediately after I hung up. I didn't check who it was before I answered because I figured it was Cali calling right back to tell me something she'd forgotten. "You've missed me so much you wanted to talk some more?" I joked as I answered the call.

"Sophia?" It was not Cali but a male voice.

"Yes?" I asked cautiously. It wasn't Luke's familiar creamy voice either, but it sounded vaguely familiar.

"Hey, it's Bradley."

"Bradley Benson?" I blurted out in surprise. "From BYU?" I'd never expected to hear from him again.

"Yeah, that Bradley. Do you know more than one?"

"Well, no." I fumbled to regain my composure. "It's just that this is such a surprise."

"Hopefully a pleasant one."

"Of course." We had dated a couple of times fall semester, but I had ended things in December. I hoped there were no hard feelings. He didn't sound like there were.

"How are you?" he asked.

"Uh, good." I was still curious about the reason for the phone call. "And you? How are you?" I said, remembering my manners.

"Great."

This wasn't getting any easier. "So where are you? Didn't you join the peace corps or something?" I grasped for a topic we could comfortably discuss. He was probably calling me from South America or someplace like that.

"Actually I'm going to be in your neck of the woods, or desert, soon."

"Really?" I squeaked. Again, not from excitement but from anticipation. Was he just passing through? Was he going to want to get together?

Or maybe more? "Do you need a place to stay?" I asked, thinking maybe that was why he was calling. I wasn't really looking to invite him to stay with us. It just kind of came out that way.

"Actually, no. I need someplace to go to church."

"Church?" I repeated.

"Yeah. I'm coming down with a few buddies to go hiking in Red Rock Canyon, camping on Mount Charleston, and boating at Lake Mead. Since you live in the area, I thought I could meet up with you for church on Sunday and say hello."

"Yeah, yeah, of course you can. That'd be great." I worried I was sounding too enthusiastic. I didn't want to give him the impression that we were anything more than friends. I told him where our church building was and when we met.

"I'll let you know when I'm coming," he said pleasantly.

"See you, Bradley," I said, distracted. Were his motives as simple as that, or were there absolutely no motives? And why was I so vain as to assume his coming down here had something to do with me? I needed a reality check. Or maybe just an ego check.

Chapter Seven

Redefine Yourself

"HEY," I SAID, STILL FEELING strange talking at my computer, even if Luke was on the other end of the conversation. We had Skyped a few times in the five days he'd been gone, but I still wasn't used to it.

"Hi." He gave me a weak smile. "How are you?"

"I'm okay," I said, reaffirming that I was. "How's the jet lag? You look tired." Maybe it was his five o'clock shadow that made him look tired. I had never seen him this unshaven, but I could get used to it. I didn't think I'd woken him up, but I also didn't think he had been awake for very long. His hair and T-shirt were both rumpled.

"Nah, I'm more or less adjusted to the time change."

"Did you go out for a jog this morning?" I asked.

"No. Just stayed up late last night, and now I'm paying for it."

"Sightseeing?"

His mouth turned down in a slight frown. "Studying."

"Studying?" I repeated. "Have you done any sightseeing?" I felt like we hadn't had a real conversation since he'd arrived. The first time he Skyped was the night he'd arrived, which had ended up being 2:00 a.m. my time because of the time difference. The next time we Skyped, it was morning where he was, and he was running late for class. This was the longest conversation we had had so far.

"The professor gave us a packet to read on the plane and quizzed us the first day of class. He hasn't let up yet." Luke let out a throaty laugh. "I wish I were sightseeing."

"Sounds . . . fun," I said.

"This program is a little more demanding than I thought it would be," he said.

"I was picturing glorified sightseeing."

"Yeah, that's what I was expecting too. Which we'll do. I mean, we'll go on tours and stuff. But the professor wants a three-page essay on five historical sites for all the cities we're going to."

I did the math quickly in my head. "So fifteen pages per city, one city per week for six weeks. So fifteen times six is—"

"Ninety pages. It's not really a big deal, but it feels like busywork. This is stuff we did in the entry-level classes."

"It's time-consuming?" I asked, feeling him out. A tight feeling was building up in my chest.

"Not if I do one report a night." He let out a big sigh. "It's just kind of ridiculous. It's like the professor needed to justify the trip by making us do something. And I haven't even thought of the final project yet."

"There's a final project?" I gulped. The course expectations kept getting worse and worse, and I felt like this was my class instead of his.

"Yeah. Left to our discretion. That almost makes it harder, you know?"

I nodded. "Sometimes it's easier to have the topic assigned."

"In this case, I think it would. And the professor is so flaky it's annoying. I mean, I don't need these credits to graduate."

"What do you mean? Are you going to UW?" I had unofficially withdrawn from a class my freshman year. My grade for the class had been bad, and I'd doubted I would pass the final, so I'd just stopped going. I hadn't realized having a *UW* on my transcript was worse than an *F* GPA-wise.

"No way. It would screw up my GPA. I have to suck it up and do the stupid busywork."

My breath came out in a "whew." "For a minute, I thought you were giving up," I said, then understood why I was feeling so uptight.

"Give up?" Luke gave a small laugh. "It's not something to give up over. I'm just griping that I have to do it. I'll get over it."

"I wish I could help," I said, feeling that urge to fix things again. "You know, whip up a couple of essays or something."

"You would do that for me?" Luke gave me a sexy smile.

"I sure would."

"Which would be awesome if you were the one earning the grade."

"You do have a point," I agreed.

"I'm going to sit down this weekend and crank out as many as I can. Maybe if I do the stupid assignments I can actually enjoy the rest of the time here instead of doing research."

"I'm sort of jealous your essays are taking time away from me," I teased.

"Yeah, well, duty calls. Part of the sacrifice of getting an education so I can get a good job."

"Oh, wait. Here, how about this," I said. I cleared my voice dramatically. "Ode to the Leaning Tower of Pisa

Almost as famous as the Mona Lisa

Some hope to fix your lean

But that would just be mean

'Cause then you'd be like any other tower."

Luke chuckled. "That's awesome, Sophia, but I don't think that's what the professor is looking for."

"No?"

Luke shook his head. "No. I'm not sure he has a sense of humor."

"Good thing I have one I can supply you with until you return."

"I'll take it," Luke said, then sighed.

"If you were Travis, you would have given up and failed the class." I already knew that Luke was a better guy, and this only reinforced it.

His face clouded momentarily. "Good thing I'm not Travis, then," he said, his voice completely flat.

I realized he hadn't taken my observation as encouragement. I knew better than to mention Travis. I backpedaled. "No, no, that's not what I meant. I mean, I did mean it, but what I meant was I'm glad you're not like Travis. Having been through all the times he gave up, I appreciate that you don't give up. Even if it's doing stupid busywork for a class you don't even need and sticking it out."

His expression softened. "So that was a compliment?"

"That's exactly how I meant it." I batted my eyes and gave a silly smile, trying to lighten the mood. "Hey," I said, wanting to get away from my conversation faux-pas. "Is that invitation still open to come visit you when you get home?"

He visibly brightened. "You want to?"

I nodded vigorously. "I'm looking forward to it."

"You are?"

"Yeah, I'm anxious to see you again."

"Yeah, me too. You could meet my mom, stay for a couple days."

"I would love to."

"She's anxious to meet you."

A thought hit me. "Does your mom know I'm, you know, divorced?" I asked. Would she even care?

"I told her a long time ago. Back when we first started dating."

We'd been dating for a long time? I guess so. By BYU standards, it was average, but in real life, it was short, and in Travis time, we would have already been married and divorced by now.

"What did she say?"

"Her exact words were, 'That poor girl,' but if it's her opinion you're worried about, she's fine with it."

That was a relief.

Luke leaned close into the computer screen and looked straight into the camera. "Divorce doesn't define you. It's just a detail."

"A big detail."

"To me it's just a detail. If anything, it's what made you who you are today. The Sophia I know and like. Maybe it's time to redefine yourself. Being divorced is not who you are. You are so much more than that. I know how painful it was for you, but I'm sort of thankful to Travis. Otherwise I would have never had my chance."

"I know you understand, but will it matter to your family?"

"Why would it matter? It's not like you're damaged goods."

Perhaps that was my problem. I thought of myself as damaged goods.

"So what do you think about visiting?" Luke brought the conversation around to the original topic, which I was grateful for.

"Sure, let's plan it," I said, knowing it might be something so much more than just a visit.

"Some of my family might even be visiting. We always get together for the Fourth of July."

I wasn't sure I was ready to meet the rest of his family yet. His mom might be enough for one visit. "Sounds . . . fun," I managed.

He was quiet for a moment. "I miss you, Soph."

"I miss you too."

"I can't wait to see you again."

I put a sappy smile on my face. "I know. I'm crossing off the days on my calendar."

"Good night, honey."

"Good night, Luke."

There was a pause, one probably meant to be filled in with "I love you" and "I love you too." Instead, we observed a moment of silence.

We logged off, and I sat there staring at the blank screen, a mess of confused emotions rushing through me. Love was so easy the first time around, when I was eighteen and naïve to the realities of it. I thought about the saying that love will conquer fear, but I was in a slightly different situation. Love had caused my fear. So what did I do about that?

The picture Luke took of us the day he left was tucked in the corner of a frame on my desk. Seeing it made my pulse quicken. There was no way I could deny I had it bad for him. I looked at it often, usually when I checked for his e-mails several times a day. We e-mailed every day unless he was traveling, and his came just after lunch, nighttime in Europe. It gave me something to look forward to.

I scrolled through Facebook and looked at Pinterest for a few minutes before checking my inbox. I was hoping he might have sent a little online good night in the last few minutes since I had spoken to him. There was nothing from him, but I did get something from Gretchen.

Hey Chickie,

So sorry to hear about everything that has happened with you and Travis. I can't believe it! I never thought you two would get divorced. I can't believe he's already remarried and to your roommate. What a weird situation that must have been.

I'm glad things are better now.

I have four weeks left. I would love to get together once I'm back. We have so much to catch up on.

Take care of yourself.

Love,

Gretch

I flopped onto my bed. Four weeks until Gretchen came home. Yay! And Luke would be home a week after her. I had a lot to look forward to. I considered my mom's words and wondered if it really would go by faster if I kept busy. I also decided to take Luke's advice and keep my chin up. I was not going to wallow in self-pity. So my boyfriend was away. Things could be worse. A year ago I was newly divorced and depressed. Life was much better now, and I had no reason to have a pity party. I wanted to keep it that way.

Chapter Eight
Decisions of Ginormous Proportions

THERE WAS NO HINT OF how the evening was going to turn out when I came home from babysitting at Cali's. It had been three weeks since the end of the semester, and I was congratulating myself for my streak of not pining. Granted, I checked my e-mail first thing in the morning when I woke up and last thing at night before I went to bed and before I showered and after I showered and before and after lunch and immediately when I got home from work. But missing Luke and being anxious to have contact with him did not, in my mind, qualify as pining. Missing, yes. Pining, no.

"Hi, Sophia," Rhonda said, interrupting my thoughts.

"Hey," I said slowly. "When did you guys get here?" I had to admit, I was surprised to find Rhonda and Ashlee sitting in the kitchen.

"About a half hour ago."

I thought hard. Did I forget they were coming or just not know? "I didn't realize you were coming this weekend. Are you staying all weekend?" I had been trying to keep busy between babysitting, crocheting, and even volunteering in my mom's classroom to prepare for the upcoming school year. And I had been asked to speak in sacrament the next Sunday, which I had thought a lot about but had not actually done anything about. With all this on my mind, I must have missed the memo about their visit.

Rhonda giggled. "It was sort of short notice and a quick visit. We're only staying until tomorrow night. Hopefully that will be long enough." Rhonda and Ashlee looked at each other and giggled again.

Sometimes they were *so* giddy. "Do you guys have big plans?"

"Hopefully." Rhonda squeeked, which turned into a laugh, which got Ashlee going again. "Dan hasn't said anything?"

I was at a loss. "About what?"

Rhonda glanced at Ashlee. "About this weekend."

"Nope." I pursed my lips and looked from Rhonda to Ashlee. "Should he have?"

Rhonda looked slightly less excited. "About his plans? He hasn't said anything to you?"

I shook my head. "I didn't even know you were coming."

"Don't worry, Rhonda. It'll still be great." Ashlee patted her on her arm. "Are you surprising him?"

"Hopefully he is surprising her," Ashlee answered.

"But he knows you're coming?" I was still completely confused.

"Yes." Rhonda nodded.

Ashlee giggled. "He was the one who proposed it."

They looked at each other and chuckled.

I did an imaginary eye roll. "Okay, well, you two have fun with whatever super girly things you're doing."

"We will," they chimed, then burst into laughter. Apparently they had eaten too many brownies or too much candy or something on the drive down here and were on a sugar high.

"I need to go check my e-mail," I said as a way of excusing myself. "I'll be back."

"Okay," Rhonda said.

I wasn't sure how soon I would be back down. I knew my parents were planning on barbequing for dinner, so I'd at least be down for that. I checked my phone for the time as I walked up the stairs: 5:20. Seven hours difference in Europe where Luke was. It would be past midnight, but Luke might be up, though I probably needed to let him sleep. He would say I hadn't woken him up if I Skyped him now, but it really was too late for him. Dang.

I passed the time by multitasking, crocheting, and thinking deep, serious thoughts, which translated into overanalyzing life in general and my relationship with Luke. Unfortunately it did not make the time go any faster.

I felt a little in limbo with where I was in life right now. I still had no idea what I wanted to do when I grew up and, as a result, had no clue what to major in. I hoped if I stayed busy some of my unknowns would work themselves out. I needed to get serious and figure them out sometime soon. I needed to move forward with my life. I just wasn't sure where forward was.

And that conversation with Luke. Redefine myself? One way to do that was to stop thinking of myself as damaged goods. I needed to get past what Travis did. It made me too conflicted over my feelings for Luke and where our relationship was going.

Just for fun and curiosity (all right, desperation), I Googled "fear of commitment" and "fear of love," hoping to find an article to help me decipher my concerns. Hopefully I was not alone and what I was feeling, or fearing, was real. I found all sorts of weird phobias. The closest I came was philophobia, the fear of love. But, really, what it came down to was realizing Luke was not Travis, though remembering that was easier said than done. Telling myself that made sense in my head and in my heart, but then thinking about telling Luke I loved him and taking things to the next level made the anxiety kick in again. I decided to stop psychoanalyzing myself, stop driving myself crazy with worry and fears, and just try to enjoy what I had with Luke when I was with him.

Again, easier said than done.

My contemplative session was abruptly interrupted a little later by Rhonda's screams.

* * *

"I said yes!" Rhonda was gushing when I hurried into the kitchen. My mom and dad were already there, my dad still holding the large metal spatula he'd been using for the barbeque.

Oh my gosh. Did Dan just propose? Suddenly all of Rhonda and Ashlee's earlier giggling conversation made sense.

Rhonda was joining our family. Dan was getting married. Rhonda becoming my sister-in-law would surely be life-altering and family-dynamic-changing. The news gave me an overwhelming need to sit down. I felt floored, although not quite as badly as when I found out Claire and Travis had eloped.

"Oh, Dan and Rhonda, that's wonderful!" My mom rushed to hug them both.

"Congratulations, son," my dad said once Mom released them. He pulled Dan into a hug and thumped his back a few times. "Welcome to the family," he said to Rhonda, hugging her next.

"Were you planning this?" I whispered into Dan's ear as I hugged him, since hugging seemed to be the thing to do at the moment. I felt out of the loop. Why hadn't Dan given me a head's up?

"I've been thinking about it for a while now. But this week I just knew."

How did he know? How does one "just know"? That was a million-dollar question for me. I wanted to just know. I thought I had just known with Travis, but look how wrong I had been.

I stepped back from him, fighting the thought that it had happened too quickly. "So, tell us all about the proposal."

Rhonda looked at Dan, her cheeks pink and her smile a thousand watts. "Do you want to tell it?"

Dan nodded at Rhonda in encouragement. "No, you go ahead and tell it."

Then they both did this nuzzle thing. Ew, ew, ew! I wasn't disgusted by them. I was disgusted because I knew I had been exactly the same way when Travis and I had gotten engaged. Dan and Rhonda had every right to be happy and excited and even grossly cheesy. This was a big moment in their lives. I took a deep breath and swallowed my revulsion.

"Well," Rhonda started, then looked to Dan, signaling his turn.

"We went up to the Las Vegas Temple," Dan said.

"And we went into the courtyard, where Dan got down on one knee and asked me to marry him." Rhonda's words came out in a rush, and she did her clapping-in-succession thing. "Then he took my shoe off and wrote in black Sharpie *Dan* on the bottom of it. You know, like Andy in *Toy Story*?"

I wondered if *Rhonda* was on the bottom of his shoe in black Sharpie.

Ashlee let out a squeal. "That is *soooo* romantic! When and where is the wedding? I want to be there."

Rhonda was still beaming. "We're not sure, but we're thinking the Las Vegas Temple the first Saturday in August."

Ooh. That would be hot. Really, really hot.

Ashlee pulled out her phone as my mom went to the calendar.

"The . . . seventh?" my mom said.

"Yup, it's the seventh," Ashlee confirmed, looking at a calendar on her screen.

"Then the seventh it is," Dan announced. Rhonda did her clapping thing again and made a squee-ing noise.

Aside from the problem (unbeknownst to Rhonda) of the searing temperatures in August, there was one other thing that had been forgotten. The seventh was my birthday. Not that I was going to have a huge party that would take up most of the day or anything, but it was still my birthday.

Instead of being happy about the date they'd picked, I was bothered by it. And I was bothered by my blatant selfishness that was pretty much staring back at me. Why couldn't I just be happy for my brother and forget about myself?

"Oh, but that's Sophia's birthday," my mom said. She turned and looked at me. "You don't mind sharing, do you? You can have two pieces of cake." She clapped her hands and had a look of complete satisfaction on her face. Apparently two pieces of cake was all it took to keep me satisfied, which might possibly be true some days, but today was not one of them.

I thought about writing to Luke about it that night in my e-mail but decided to follow my earlier urge to Skype him instead. This news was worthy of a Skype session.

* * *

Once I had connected with Luke, I dispensed with the greetings and jumped right into the topic of Rhonda and Dan's wedding. "I can't believe it. I knew it was serious but not this serious."

"That is generally what happens with couples once they have been dating awhile." Luke seemed mildly amused.

"But married? Rhonda will be my sister-in-law. What if she and my mom gang up on me?"

"You might have to wear an apron and make homemade dinner rolls," Luke said. "I think you would rock the apron, and I would never turn down homemade dinner rolls."

I looked at him, my brow furrowed.

"But domesticity is not the topic, is it?" he said quickly.

I shrugged one shoulder and then both. "I mean, I guess I figured they would probably get married. One day. Not any time soon though."

Luke opened his mouth to respond, but I cut him off. "I know everyone's going to think I'm jealous that they're getting married . . ."

"Is it the marriage thing? 'Cause if you're jealous, we can get married tomorrow."

I looked at Luke's expression to see if he was joking. I was pretty sure he was. He was, wasn't he? Was he hinting at something? I smiled even though I felt a little squeamish. "You'd fly halfway across the world to marry me tomorrow?" I really needed to clarify.

"Well, I might not get there tomorrow, but I'd be on a plane in a heart-beat. Then we could go to the Strip the next day . . ." His face finally broke into a smile.

I wondered if he could see my huge sigh of relief. "Let's not. I prefer the traditional way of getting married."

"Oh, you do, do you?"

We were getting *way* off course. "Hey, don't change the subject."

"Sorry. You distracted me. What were we talking about?"

"Rhonda and Dan getting married."

He nodded. "That's right."

"I'm not jealous that they're getting married. And did I mention it's on my birthday? Is it completely petty of me to be bothered, or what?"

"I don't think so, Soph. It's nice to have your birthday be your day."

"Yeah, maybe." I shrugged, though I didn't totally agree. I wasn't quite sure what was bothering me so much. Maybe just everything.

"Hey, sweetie?" Luke said.

It made my stomach flutter the way he said it.

"Yeah?"

"I wish you were here in Paris with me right now."

Was he distracting me? Because it was working. "I'd be happy to be anywhere with you right now. Paris, Vegas. It's not where I am but who I am with that makes it special."

"I know what you mean. I totally know what you mean." He gave me a smile that melted my heart.

Chapter Nine
Just Ashlee

I WENT DOWNSTAIRS AFTER MY visit with Luke. The air was still electrified with the news. Dan and Rhonda were on the phone with her family. My mom was hovering over Dan. She was probably waiting for her chance to talk to Rhonda's mom. Or maybe she was just waiting for them to get off the phone so she and Rhonda could get to what they loved best: planning a party.

As soon as Rhonda hung up, she and Dan left to go ring shopping. Despite all the excitement, I couldn't help but notice Ashlee was not her usual, chipper self.

"Are you okay, Ashlee?" I would have thought it would be the other way around. I expected her to be so excited about Rhonda's getting married that she'd be obnoxious.

She thought for a moment, then her eyes teared up a bit. "I feel like I'm losing Rhonda."

I guided her to the living room, and we sat down on the couch. "You mean because she's getting married? She's still going to be your friend."

She flapped her hands in front of her eyes. "I know, I know, and I'm happy for her. But I'm going to miss her being my roommate."

For me, it was not so much losing a roommate as it was gaining a sister-in-law. I would have given Ashlee that trade if I could. "Maybe you should have set her up with your brother instead," I joked lightly. She did have a brother, didn't she? I tried to remember.

"That would never have happened."

I must have been wrong about the brother. "What do you mean?"

"I'm the only member of the Church in my family. I got baptized when I was fifteen. My parents still aren't very happy about it. So they probably wouldn't be too keen on my sixteen-year-old brother marrying a twenty-year-old Mormon girl."

"Yeah, that would put a bad spin on BYU cougar, huh?" I laughed at my own joke.

Ashlee smiled a tiny bit.

"Your parents still aren't happy even though it's been three years?"

"No. My dad was so mad about my decision to come to Utah he told me not to come home."

I had no idea. I didn't know what to say. "I'm sorry."

She shrugged. "I'm used to starting over. My dad was in the military, so we moved around a lot. I was always the new kid. I learned quickly it was easier to be outgoing and make friends than to not."

Again, I knew none of this. "Wow. I thought it was tough when I got rezoned to a different high school for one year. Does your family still move a lot?"

"No. My dad retired about five years ago, and we stayed in Texas. But even though he's retired, he runs his life and his family like he's still in the military. It's kind of nice to be on my own and not living under such strict rules anymore. I chose a hair school around BYU because I wanted to be in a good environment where people supported my beliefs."

I realized how mature Ashlee was to know that and choose it. I took for granted that I had a good, supportive family who all had the same standards and beliefs. What if Ashlee had been the one who'd come to BYU, gotten married and divorced at eighteen, and had to beg her parents to let her return home in shame? Would her family have supported her like mine had? Would they have blamed her religion for the disintegration of her marriage? Would they have guilted and blamed her instead of loving her? "So you're not going back home anytime soon?"

"My parents will eventually calm down," Ashlee said.

"When? In ten years?" I was shocked about Ashlee's situation and how little I knew about her. Apparently I wasn't the only one who kept my past to myself.

"My dad just needs to get used to the idea. Plus, my school program is a year, so I'll go visit once I'm done. Things should be back to normal by then."

"You don't miss them?" My mom frequently overwhelmed me with her PMA, but I knew that if I needed to, I could come home in a heartbeat and count on her support. I couldn't imagine not having my parents' support.

She shrugged. "Don't get me wrong, I love my family, but home life is a tough situation. Aside from my dad being so strict, I have two brothers who have ADD really bad. They require a lot of patience, and since I'm the oldest, I was responsible when my parents couldn't be. I babysat a lot. It's kind of nice to be here and living my own life. For the first time ever, I can be just Ashlee."

And suddenly I felt like I was eating a large slice of humble pie. I had judged Ashlee all wrong.

She continued without my even prompting her. "I came here and met Rhonda, and she was so fun, and for once in my life, I could just have fun."

All the pieces fell into place, and with one short conversation, I learned more about Ashlee than I had known in almost six months. It made her instantly less obnoxious than she had been before. I understood her relationship with Rhonda better and why she was sad about Rhonda's marriage.

"Ashlee, I'm really impressed. I know you'll miss Rhonda, but you are obviously a strong person, and you'll be okay."

She made a pouty face. "Easy for you to say. You'll have Rhonda all the time."

I literally could not stop myself from laughing. "Let's just say Rhonda and I don't have the bond you two have, and I would never be able to replace you."

"You really think so?"

"I know so." I gave her a hug and vowed to be kinder and more understanding with her from now on. She had her own tough road to travel.

Chapter Ten
Green (with Envy) Is Not My Color

"LOOK! LOOK!" RHONDA RUSHED UP to me when she and Dan returned. "I got my ring." She held her hand out for me to inspect it.

It was a quarter-carat, marquee-cut diamond on a plain gold band—way less dramatic in size and bling than what Travis had given me. My brother had only been out of college for a year and was still paying off student loans. It wasn't like he could afford something really fancy.

"Pretty," I said, looking at it. I almost said "cute," but no one wanted their wedding ring to be cute.

"I know. Isn't it beautiful?" Rhonda pulled her hand from mine and looked at it again.

I hadn't thought about it until now, but I should have offered them my old ring. But who wanted a hand-me-down wedding ring?

"I am so happy," she exclaimed, then threw her arms around my brother's neck. She kissed him on his mouth, three times. I could deal with all the talk about the engagement, but the amount of mush was a little gross. I wasn't used to my brother being mushy. And with Rhonda, no less. Had I been this obnoxious? I *really* owed Gretchen a *huge* apology.

I escaped to Cali's house.

"You're an hour early," Cali said as she opened the door.

"Dan and Rhonda just got engaged. It's . . ."

"What?" Cali waited.

"I needed a break. Hope you don't mind."

"Not as long as you don't mind that I'm trying to clean up."

"Feel free to pretend I'm not even here," I said, taking a seat.

"Are you happy about it?"

"Yes, I am happy for both of them. But truth be told, I'm a little jealous."

"Jealous?"

I couldn't believe I was admitting this. "Yes. Green with envy."

Cali stopped what she was doing and looked right at me. "Why?"

I took a deep breath. "I'm not jealous that they're getting married. I'm jealous of their innocent love. I wish I could go back to trusting blindly in love." Unfortunately I knew things could go wrong in a relationship and love wasn't guaranteed. My relationship with Luke would be so different without my divorce baggage. I wouldn't be so afraid of taking a chance at love, but I also wouldn't know how delicate it could be either.

Cali came over and sat down next to me. "That has got to be tough."

"I don't want to be this way," I said quietly. "I really am happy for them." It was less than attractive behavior. It was nice to see my brother so happy, which made me even more frustrated that I couldn't just get over myself and be more tolerant of them.

"It's hard once you've lost trust in something to be able to believe in it again. But I think it is possible, Sophia."

"How?" I asked, feeling slightly defeated. This whole trust thing had been plaguing me for too long now.

"I don't have a magical answer for that," Cali said as she put her hand on my arm. "Just like grieving, it's a process. Sometimes it's hard doing the thing that scares you the most."

Trusting in love, trusting myself, trusting Luke—I couldn't decide which one scared me the most.

* * *

When I returned from babysitting later in the day, Rhonda and Dan were working on wedding plans. They were sitting at the kitchen table, their chairs so close I would have thought it'd be uncomfortable with all the elbow bumping and knee knocking. Rhonda kept looking down at her ring and holding out her hand to admire it. I had done the same exact thing.

"How about a cheesecake wedding cake?" Rhonda suggested.

I was behind her, standing in the doorway. I stifled a laugh, then mouthed *no* and shook my head at Dan. I didn't know if Dan saw my warning or knew how enthusiastic Rhonda was about cheesecake. When I was roommates with Rhonda, she seemed to make cheesecake on a weekly basis.

"There's a bakery here that makes an awesome Bundt cake. It's the most incredible cake," he countered.

"I wanted something more traditional. You know, layers, flowers, decorations."

My brother frowned slightly. "But I thought you wanted cheesecake? That's not traditional."

"You can't stack Bundt cakes on top of each other. It would look weird."

I shook my head in bewilderment and went to the fridge to grab a Diet Coke. Sadly we were all out of cold ones, so I went into the pantry to restock the fridge. When I returned, they were making out right there at the kitchen table, in the open where anyone could walk in on them. Anyone like, say for instance, my mother, who would have been appalled. I should know.

"All right, kids, that's enough of that. You have parents living here who might possibly catch you, and that would be awkward. I'm sure they don't want to watch it either."

They detached themselves from each other's faces.

"You're just jealous, little sis," Dan said.

"No, I'm not. I have no desire to kiss Rhonda." I smirked at them and retreated back to my room. I stayed there the rest of the evening, crocheting what started out as hot pads, then turned into a baby blanket, which was becoming something more of a throw blanket. Whatever it ended up being, I could probably use it as a wedding gift for them.

* * *

My hiding-in-the-bedroom plan must not have fooled my mother. "Sophia, you need to think a little more positively," she announced brightly the next morning.

Which translated into PMA can fix anything. My suspicion was now on high alert. Since I wasn't hanging out with everyone, my mom must have gotten the impression that I needed something to do. I didn't need something more to do. I needed to adjust my attitude.

"Don't worry, I have things to do. I'm not curling up in a fetal position and staying in bed all day." I may have been missing Luke, but I wasn't having a depression relapse. I held up my crocheting. "See? I have a hobby. I crochet." I smiled brightly. I'd crocheted about a billion things since Luke had been gone. If Rhonda had wanted a crocheted wedding gown, I would have had it done in no time. After spending last night in my room on a pathetic crocheting marathon, I knew I needed to diversify the ways I spent my free time.

"Let me rephrase that: you need to do something with yourself."

"I do have something to do. I babysit. I'm listening to you, doing what you suggested, Mom." I gave her a wide smile, but I still wasn't sure where she was going with this. Something was lurking behind this conversation.

"Yes, but you need something more to do. You have too much time on your hands. Maybe you could volunteer."

"Volunteer?" I thought I had been doing that. You know, setting up her classroom. I resisted taking on any more commitments. "I don't know, maybe."

"Tyler Powers is coming home from his mission soon. Maybe you could call Sister Powers and see if she needs any help getting ready. With six kids still at home, she might need a little help."

Tyler Powers. Oh yeah, it was about time for him to be returning. He and I had gone out a few times before his mission and my first semester at college. In my mind, we'd been hanging out. In his mind, I was pretty sure we'd been dating. I didn't know how to say no nicely to him at the time. That was before Travis inadvertently forced me to learn how to stand up for myself. Plus, my mom was always in my ear, reminding me that I should give everyone a chance.

I had told him I would write to him while he was on his mission because it was something I felt I *should* do to be nice. He wrote me weekly from the time he entered the MTC in July. I had managed to write him once while he was there and once in August because he had sounded a little lonely, but keeping in touch with him went by the wayside once I arrived at BYU and started to see what a fun social life I could have. Then Travis came and swept me away, and I literally forgot about Tyler. He wrote me in September, asking if I would wait for him, but by then I was already serious with Travis. I sent him a quick note saying I'd met someone, it was getting serious, and I was sorry. After that I never thought of him again. Talk about being ashamed of myself.

"Anyway, you are not going to mope around waiting for Luke to get home. Idle hands result in—"

"Oh, and I have to work on my talk that I'm giving on Sunday. That'll keep me plenty busy." Especially since I hadn't even started it yet. I wasn't moping. I was lying low. Obviously I was failing at it.

"I don't mean just the next couple of days. I mean something a little more involved."

Lying low was slightly boring, but it was much less annoying than watching Dan and Rhonda be all lovey-dovey. Besides, Gretchen was coming home in a couple weeks, and then Luke would be home a couple days after that. I focused on those points and kept myself busy planning my travel arrangements to visit them. I could make it through the next couple of weeks.

"You know you don't even have to look that far. There is someone right in front of you who could use your help," my mom said gently.

"I guess I could call Sister Powers," I conceded.

"I am thinking of someone else."

"Who?" Was I so involved in myself that I was missing something that obvious? Then I understood. "You need some help?" I hadn't even considered that maybe my mom needed help. She was always so organized and on top of things, she rarely got overwhelmed. She was compassionate service leader, which was right up her alley. It was her *calling* to know everything about everyone. I think secretly she sort of loved it. Was there someone else in the ward, like Cali, who my mom thought I could help?

"No, not me. Rhonda."

"Rhonda?" I said, surprised. "Oh." The word stuck in my throat. I wasn't really looking to volunteer with *that*. I thought it was perfectly understandable and excusable if I didn't offer my help with their wedding.

"She would probably like some help planning things. I think it would mean a lot to her if she had your help."

I shook my head. "She likes planning that kind of stuff. I wouldn't be of any help to her."

"Sophia. That is what you want to believe. You know a wedding is a lot of work, and I bet there is some way you could help."

"Okay, I'll ask her," I said. I wasn't going to convince myself it wouldn't be bad. I tried to think of it in terms of blessings I'd receive and could probably use. Maybe I could get an advance on those blessings and get help with the talk for church I still needed to write.

Once my mom left, instead of working on my talk like I needed to, I Skyped Luke.

"You look less than thrilled," he said after I explained the situation.

"My mom sort of voluntold me to help Rhonda with the wedding."

"I take it you don't want to?"

I sighed. "I'm willing, I guess. It's hard being around them when they are so . . . gushy."

"Obnoxious?" Luke rephrased.

"Yeah." I didn't want to admit to Luke that I was jealous. I wished I could go back to the innocent state they were in, trusting love would make marriage perfect. I wasn't proud of my jealousy. "And I'm not an expert because I've planned one wedding. It's . . ."

"Because it's not yours?" Luke asked.

I shook my head. "It's just that . . ." I trailed off. If I told Luke why, it would start a discussion about our relationship that I wasn't ready to get into yet. "It's everything. It's them, it's missing you, it's . . . I don't know."

"You won't have to miss me much longer. I'm coming home soon. You're still planning on visiting, right?"

"Of course I am. That's the highlight of my summer."

"Good. I'm looking forward to seeing you again."

"Me too." I probably sounded a little giddy.

"I've been thinking," Luke said.

"Uh-oh, that might be dangerous," I joked.

"I think when I get back we should talk."

"Because we're not talking now?" It was a feeble attempt at making the conversation less intense.

He looked so serious. "This is a talk we should have in person."

My pulse quickened. "Why?" In one word, my voice went from fun and flirty to serious.

"I've been thinking about a lot of things since I've been away, and I just think we need to talk."

We need to talk. The four dreaded words. I hated those words.

Chapter Eleven
Where's a Bolt of Lightning When I Need One?

IF THE BISHOPRIC IN MY home ward had known about the last time I'd been asked to speak in my student ward, they probably wouldn't have taken their chances on me. In the student ward, I'd told them no, but I'd shown up at church only to find my name listed as the third speaker on the program anyway. Instead of scrambling to come up with a talk, I went AWOL. But gamble this bishopric did, and I was assigned the topic of King Benjamin's sermon.

Dan coached me as we walked into church Sunday morning. "People always remember the first and last thing you say. Don't get up there and admit how nervous or unprepared you feel. Say you're excited or have prepared a great talk, and people will already feel like it's a great talk. It's a trick I used on my mission."

"Or I could picture everyone in their underwear," I joked.

"You could do that too," Dan agreed. "Might not be all that attractive though."

"Or pray for a bolt of lightning to strike."

"As long as it doesn't hit you, sure, why not?" Dan said with brotherly love.

I took a deep breath, still trying to convince myself I'd do okay. "I'll be fine. I'm prepared. I'll get through it. It's only ten minutes. Right? Unless I pass out, how bad could it be?"

"I had a friend pass out at the podium. He locked his knees and fell straight backward."

"Not helping, Dan. Not helping."

"You'll do fine, Sophia, or you'll faint. Either way, this too shall pass." Dan gave me a pat on the back and left me sitting alone on the stand, staring at the daunting congregation.

There is a blessing and a curse to being the third speaker. The blessing is that time usually runs out, allowing the speaker to cut their talk short. The curse is that they have to sit through the whole meeting dreading their turn. When my turn arrived, I made my way to the podium, my legs feeling like Jell-O.

"Good afternoon," I began. My voice sounded shaky. "I am so excited about my talk today," I said woodenly, still hoping there might be a slim chance of a lightning strike. I was only able to start my talk because I knew my opening verbatim from having practiced it so many times. The words on the page swam in front of my eyes. Maybe I was even more nervous than I'd thought.

"My topic is King Benjamin's discourse." I willed myself to breathe, to speak, to concentrate on getting through. But I couldn't concentrate. I kept thinking the one person who needed to hear this talk wasn't here. Travis. When I wrote my talk, I kind of imagined him being in the congregation and did it according to what I thought he needed to hear. He was one person who could take some friendly advice from the prophet king.

I cleared my throat and started back up. "King Benjamin was a kind and just leader. He was full of wisdom. At the time he gave this sermon, he knew he was going to die soon and wanted to remind his people about the importance of doing good."

I grabbed the edges of the podium to stop my hands from shaking. I glanced up only to see Bradley Benson, flanked by two guys, walk into the chapel and take a seat on one of the benches on the side. Why was he here?

I looked down at my paper and realized I had lost my place. I desperately searched for where I had left off.

My eyes fixated on Mosiah 4:30, which had been highlighted and rehighlighted a number of times in my scriptures. It had brought me much comfort in the days immediately after my divorce. "King Benjamin warned: 'But this much I can tell you, that if ye do not watch yourselves, and your thoughts, and your words, and your deeds, and observe the commandments of God, and continue in the faith of what ye have heard concerning the coming of our Lord, even unto the end of your lives, ye must perish. And now, O man, remember, and perish not.'"

I had a sticky note stuck under that verse, and I blurted out without thinking, "Which we are also warned about in Alma 12:14–15: 'For our words will condemn us, yea, all our works will condemn us; we shall not be found spotless; and our thoughts will also condemn us; and in this awful state we shall not dare to look up to our God; and we would fain be glad if we could command the rocks and the mountains to fall upon us to hide us from his presence.

"'But this cannot be; we must come forth and stand before him in his glory, and in his power, and in his might, majesty, and dominion, and acknowledge to our everlasting shame that all his judgments are just.'" Again, another verse that brought me much consolation in those dark days.

"Our everyday thoughts and actions, though small, add up in the long run. The Lord is not the one who is going to condemn us. We condemn ourselves."

Oh. My. Gosh. I stopped, feeling like the wind had gotten knocked out of me. I realized what I had just said. I was condemning myself. All my anger and hatred for Travis. My ill-wishes for him in his marriage. I would have to answer for it. Did I really want to be that kind of person? Travis would have to answer for his actions, and I for mine. I needed to stop worrying about what I thought he deserved and try to not let the bitterness seep into my life. Or my bitterness about how he'd affected my love life seep into my relationship with Luke.

But not only that, there was my attitude toward Rhonda and Dan. It wasn't that I was being blatantly rude. I wasn't meaning to. But I wasn't exactly excited for them or even supportive. My brother had been incredibly supportive of me last summer after my divorce. It was my turn to help him.

And Ashlee. I hadn't been very understanding of her before she explained her situation. I shouldn't have to walk in someone else's shoes in order to be kind to them.

I was having an instant personal inventory, and I was coming up lacking.

I looked out into the congregation and met Dan's puzzled expression. I sounded discombobulated, and I couldn't get a complete sentence out without stumbling over the words or pausing way too long between thoughts.

Get it together, I told myself. My talk was veering dangerously off track, like heading for a train wreck.

Maybe I could do some damage control and rein in the talk, but the talk I'd meant to give had suddenly taken on a whole new meaning. "Those sound like strong words, but it is to warn us and remind us how easy it is to become lax with our everyday dealings with others. As hard as that sounds, we are given an out; we can humble ourselves and repent.

King Benjamin's whole message was about humility, reminding us how we are nothing by ourselves." I wanted to sum up my talk and sit down as quickly as possible.

I was blessed. Time was running out, and I was running out of things to say, so I was in no way complaining about ending abruptly. I looked at the clock for effect. "Time is running short, so I will close." I took a deep breath, finished, and retreated to my seat, relieved the experience was over. At least the talk part was over.

Dan waited for me at the pew. "That was really . . . passionate." He gave me a pat on the shoulder, probably in sympathy.

"Um, thanks?" I said, feeling self-conscious about my random tangent.

"What was that all about?" Dan asked.

"I got distracted and tried to recover, but I don't know if I managed to or not." I ran my hand through my hair.

"It was like all of a sudden you just stopped. Like . . ."

"Like I realized in the middle of my talk that that talk wasn't for anyone's benefit but my own?"

Dan nodded knowingly. "Oh. One of those moments."

I motioned toward the back of the chapel. "And Bradley Benson walked in during my talk."

"Who?" Dan scanned the crowd.

"Bradley Benson. He was in my BYU ward."

"Two-timing on Luke, are you?" Dan said.

I was slightly annoyed he would insinuate such a thing. Maybe I was just overly sensitive about how I treated others after the talk I'd just given.

"Nah, it's not like that with Bradley." As I said it, I hoped it was true.

"Ha! That's what you said about Luke when he came to visit over Christmas. Remember what I said? A guy's not going to make the trip unless it's worth his effort."

"Yeah, but Bradley wasn't coming to Vegas to visit me. He just called to find a ward to go to while he was here."

My brother raised an eyebrow. "That's what LDS.org is for." Considering my brother was a guy who never dated much, he was amazingly dead-on for the rules of attraction for guys, but I was sure he was wrong in this case.

Chapter Twelve
The Like Triangle

I WALKED OVER TO WHERE Bradley was waiting. After he'd called, I hadn't heard back from him, so I wasn't expecting his visit, or more accurately, I wasn't sure what he was expecting from the visit. I was still annoyed at myself for even assuming he might have expectations. For all I knew, he had moved on with his life, and I was nothing more than a friend to visit in passing. My heart didn't skip a beat as I walked up to him, but my anticipation might have climbed up a notch when he hugged me.

"Hey there, Sophia."

"Hey, Bradley." I hugged him back.

"These are my two friends, Toby and Lincoln." He pointed to his buddies.

"Hi. Nice to meet you guys." I shook their hands, then looked back at Bradley. "How was your weekend? Did you get all your stuff in?"

"Yeah." Bradley's face lit up with enthusiasm. "We even decided to go skydiving while we were here."

"Skydiving?" I swallowed. It was one more reason why I knew it was the right thing to do to not pursue a relationship.

All three guys nodded their heads in confirmation, grinning.

"And you liked jumping out of an airplane?" The very thought made my stomach knot up.

"What a rush, man," Toby said.

"And you just decided to do this? On a whim?" It would take me years to build up enough courage to hurl myself out of a moving plane thousands of feet up in the air.

"Yeah. Lincoln"—Bradley nodded toward him—"has a friend who works for one of the skydiving companies in Boulder City, so he was able to hook us up. It was a *total* rush."

"Let's just say that is one rush I am in no rush to experience."

"Sophia, are you still avoiding pushing your limits?" Bradley said, and the three guys chuckled.

"What can I say? I like to play it safe." Like with my relationship with Luke. Ah-ha! I guess I *was* doing that with him, huh?

"Hey, we're going to Sunday School," Toby said to Bradley, then looked at me. "It was nice to meet you."

"The same," Lincoln said.

"Yeah, sure. Nice meeting you guys too." I smiled and half waved as they walked off.

Bradley touched my elbow. "You look different, Sophia."

"I do?" I stepped back. He didn't look different, except for his tan, which made his eyes bluer and added to his swoon appeal.

"Yeah. I'm not even sure what it is. Did you change your hair? Lose weight? Not that you needed to lose weight, but something is different."

I'm happy, I thought. I didn't look and feel so tragic anymore. "Nope, I didn't change anything." It was time. Time changed everything. A year ago I hadn't thought that was even possible.

"Sophia?" someone from behind me asked.

I turned around to see Tyler, fresh off his mission, and I realized I never had called his mom. "Tyler? You're done serving your time?" I didn't mean to make it sound like a prison sentence. It felt more like I had been the one serving time.

He puffed his chest. "Yes. Finished. Completed. Returned with honor."

"Wow." I didn't know what to say. I didn't want to sound shallow by admitting I had completely stopped thinking about him. "It went by . . . quick." Hopefully for him. "I didn't see you in sacrament meeting."

He nodded. "I reported to the stake presidency this morning, and it ran late."

I let out a deep breath. "Oh, that makes sense." I realized Bradley was still standing next to me. "Um, this is Bradley. Bradley, this is Tyler."

They shook hands, but there was no comradery in it.

Tyler continued as if Bradley wasn't even there. "I heard from a friend of a friend that you were home."

"Yup. Break from school," I said. "That's where I met Bradley." I felt the need to include him in the conversation since I had been talking with him first.

"Is he your husband?" I saw Tyler do a quick ring check.

I choked on my spit.

"Husband?" Bradley was obviously surprised.

"Sophia?" Cali's voice rang out from the other entrance of the chapel. She must have seen us and come to join the little party.

"Wait. I'm confused," Bradley broke in. "You're married?" Now he did a ring check.

"No, no. I'm divorced."

Bradley blinked. "You've gotten married and divorced since the last time I saw you?"

"No. That was from before."

"Before?" Bradley said. I could tell he was still confused.

Cali reached us. "Is this Luke?" she asked, then looked at Bradley. "You're not Luke."

Bradley looked at her weird. "No, I'm Bradley."

"Oh." Cali looked thoughtful, then set her sights on Tyler.

Please realize he's not Luke. Please realize he's not Luke. Please don't say any more, please, please, please . . .

"You're . . ." Cali asked, looking at Tyler and waiting.

"Tyler Powers."

"And you're Bradley?" Cali was trying to process who these guys were.

"I'm confused," Tyler announced. Join the club. Confusion seemed to be a way of life for me lately. "You're still divorced, and he's not your husband?"

"I didn't even know she was divorced," Bradley said.

I faced Tyler. "Yes. No. Okay, wait. I know Bradley from school. We were in the same ward." Then I turned to Bradley. "I know Tyler from this ward. He just got home from his mission."

"We dated before I left," Tyler added.

I decided now was not the time to establish where he and I stood relationship-wise. That was something to be discussed in private.

"And where does divorce fit in?" Bradley asked.

"My first year at college I got married and divorced."

"But now you're single?" Tyler asked.

Oh no. Was *he* trying to establish where we stood relationship-wise?

"Well, yeah, single as in not married." I didn't want to bring up or discuss my relationship with Luke at the moment. I didn't want to be presumptuous that Tyler was still interested in me, but I also wanted to be preemptive.

"And who is Luke?" Bradley asked. If he was trying not to appear too interested, he was failing.

"I've been dating him." I could tell Bradley the details later if necessary.

"Wow, look at the time," Cali said, talking loudly and not even caring how obvious she was being. "Are you going to Sunday School?" She gave us all a pointed look.

We nodded, but no one moved.

"C'mon, kids." Cali was shameless as she began corralling us from the chapel. Finally Tyler started to shuffle out.

"Awkward," Cali whispered in passing as she took the lead.

"Yeah," I whispered back.

I followed Cali, thankful to escape the like triangle. Bradley silently walked next to me on one side, Tyler on the other. I expected Bradley to find his friends once we were in Sunday School, but he stuck by my side. Tyler veered off and sat with his parents. I self-consciously walked to the front of the room to sit with my parents and Dan on the third row. Right where everyone could see us.

"What about your friends?" I whispered to Bradley.

"I'm ditching them so I can sit with you." He winked and sat down beside me.

"They're not going to miss you?"

"They'll survive."

During the lesson, Bradley handed me a piece of paper.

So you and Tyler dated?

I wouldn't exactly call it that. We were more like friends.

I don't think that poor guy knows it.

I drew a smiley face.

You never said anything about being married. You were like eighteen. How?

Nineteen. I had just turned nineteen when I met you. I was at BYU the year before and got married my first semester. After four months, Travis decided he wanted a divorce. When you met me, I was still a mess.

So it wasn't that you weren't interested in me? It was just bad timing?

I couldn't come out and say I wasn't interested in him. That was hurtful. But I still stuck by my opinion that we were too different to date. And I didn't want to date him. I had Luke, and Luke was the one I wanted to be with.

Yeah, it was a very bad time.

But you're doing better?

Much better.

So what's going on with this guy Luke?

I squirmed in my seat. How exactly to define it? *We're sort of in a relationship. It's complicated.*

Sort of? Either you are or you're not.

True, when it was stated that way. But it really was complicated, and I didn't owe Bradley an explanation. I had already made my choice. *I am.*

You are?

Yes.

Is it serious? Or do I have a chance?

No, he didn't have a chance. Was it serious? I knew the answer was yes. I just didn't want to admit that the answer was yes. Wasn't that why Luke and I were in an "it's complicated" situation right now? Because I couldn't admit how I felt for him? I admitted as much as I could let myself admit. *It's on its way to being serious.* Well, on its way, depending on how you qualified "serious."

Do I still have a chance?

Bradley . . . He took the paper back before I could finish writing.

You're a hard one to give up on.

Why would he say that or think that? I was certainly no prize back when I knew him at school.

Like I said before, I think we are two different people. You need a girl who knows how to ride a bike, won't sprain her ankle hiking, and is willing to jump out of an airplane with you. That's just not me.

I thought you were playing the damsel in distress.

I was in distress—it wasn't an act—and I was trying to get over a guy, not get a guy. I don't know if you realized it, but there were plenty of girls in the ward who were in distress over you. :)

But your distress was very attractive.

I'm not so sure about that, but it was nice of you to say so. And despite your creative effort, I am not the right girl for you. I'm sorry.

I want to make sure I have tried everything possible so I know I tried.

I processed his last sentence. "You have tried," I whispered. "Honestly, you couldn't have done anything differently. But Luke and I . . ."

"Were you dating him at school?" Bradley asked.

My mother shot me a look to shush.

"We started dating after you graduated." This was not the conversation I really wanted to be having during Sunday School. I didn't want to have this conversation at all.

"How did you meet him?"

I looked away from my mother's gesture to cut it out. "He's Luke James, the elders quorum president in our singles ward."

"You and Luke?" Bradley nodded as he soaked in the information.

"Yes. Luke and me."

"He knew you were divorced?" Bradley looked curious.

"The whole ward knew I was divorced once Rhonda found out."

Bradley smiled a little, then leaned forward and ducked his head down. "And now you and Luke are dating?"

I had no choice but to lean forward too. "Yes."

"And you say it's serious?"

I nodded yes, owning it.

"So I guess after church today it will really be good-bye?"

I tried whispering more quietly. "For what it's worth, Bradley, I'm sorry."

"Well, at least I tried."

"I'll give you that," I said softly.

Okay, Gretchen, Cali, and now Bradley and Tyler. I kept looking around for affirmation for my feelings for Luke, but did I need any more people to point out the obvious to me?

Besides, in a competition of Bradley versus Luke, I'd choose Luke. I had already chosen him.

* * *

"So who was that Bradley guy and how does he fit into your life?" Cali asked as she opened her front door on Tuesday morning. I knew Cali was not going to let me off the hook without an explanation. My mom had done the same thing at church the first moment she'd had a chance to pull me aside.

"Just a guy," I said quickly. "Am I taking Joy to playgroup today?"

"Don't think you can ignore my question. I am a lawyer. I will get it out of you." She smiled nicely, but there was a fierceness in the way she said it.

I sighed. I knew there was no way to sidestep it. "Bradley was in my BYU ward my first semester back. We went out a couple times, if that's what you want to call it, but I managed to botch it up."

"How did you do that?"

"He's very outdoorsy, and even though he's cute and very eligible, I'm not the right girl for him. We have very different interests."

Cali seemed disappointed that there wasn't more to the story. "Well, I guess it's good that you didn't date him just for amusement."

"I wasn't looking to have a boy toy."

"I don't know, it might have been fun just for a little bit." Cali shrugged. "I mean, if I was nineteen again and not happily married." She chuckled.

I frowned slightly. "I couldn't use him just to have some fun and provide a distraction. I'm not that type of person, and at the time, it would have taken too much energy."

She leaned in a little closer. "So why did he visit?"

"He was in town with some friends, skydiving and hiking and stuff."

"Did he think you were going to get together for a date or something?"

"When he called, he wanted to meet me for church. But he was putting feelers out, wondering if there was a chance."

"Is there?"

I shook my head to emphasize my point. "No, and I told him that."

"Is he completely clear with it though?"

"Yes," I confirmed. "He is."

Chapter Thirteen
It's Always Good to Have Two Thighs

MY MOTHER HAS A MAGNET on her fridge that reads, "Good friends are like thighs; they always stick together." That was how I felt about Gretchen's return. I felt like a part of me was returning. Being totally wrapped up in Travis had made me forget what a great friend she was. With her return, we could pick up the friendship where it had left off.

I talked to her the day after she got home, and we made plans for me to visit her that next weekend. I had also Skyped Luke, who was returning from Europe the same day I was driving to Gretchen's. From Gretchen's house in Temecula, I was going to his house for a couple of days. I hadn't talked to him for more than five-minute increments since the "We Need to Talk" conversation. I'd been a nervous wreck since then. He'd asked me a few times if something was wrong or if I was upset with him, but I always avoided the answer. Knowing we needed to have a conversation made me anxious about visiting him.

Cali was kind enough to let me take her car in exchange for driving her and her husband and baby to the airport for their vacation. It was more than a fair trade on her part, in my mind.

So off to California I went. I couldn't wait to see Gretchen. In reality, I couldn't wait to see Luke either, but I was more than willing to put off *the talk*.

* * *

"Sophia! Yay! You're here," Gretchen exclaimed when she opened her front door. She was one of those girls who had a soft voice and was always so sincere.

"Gretchen!" I said, dropping my bag so I could hug her. She looked the same. She was a petite 5'4", especially when compared to me, her straight black hair still cut at her shoulders and her signature freckles splaying out across her nose.

"C'mon in. I'm the only one home right now." Gretchen gestured to me with a wave. She was an only child, and I assumed her parents were at work. She led me into the living room, where we sat on the overstuffed couch.

"Look at you! How are you?" I said.

"Great." Her eyes were bright with enthusiasm.

"How is it being home?" I wondered how she felt. People returning home from their missions always describe the feeling as weird. Was it as weird as I'd felt when I'd gone home soon-to-be divorced?

"I don't really know what to do with myself. I feel like I should be doing something instead of relaxing, you know? I miss being there and feel out of place here."

"I know the feeling. Are you glad you went?"

"For sure. It was such a unique experience. It was hard but good at the same time. It's hard to explain. Going door to door, knocking, trying to find people to teach, that was hard. But when we did have people to teach, it was good. When the weather was miserable, that was hard, but when we had an amazing spiritual experience, that was good. If I had a hard companion or elders who were immature or just drove me nuts or an area with struggling members, that was hard. But if I had a great companion, with great elders, in a great area with great ward members, it was wonderful. There are some lessons I learned on my mission that I don't think I could have learned any other way."

"I know what you mean." The lessons I'd learned going through my divorce probably couldn't have been learned otherwise. I had changed a lot because of the divorce.

Gretchen continued. "It wasn't all bad. I would say the good definitely outweighed the bad. The thing that was the hardest for me was when I had a companion I didn't click with and I couldn't get away from her. There was no reprieve."

"That would be tough." At least when I was married I could still have time away from Travis, especially if we were fighting.

Gretchen nodded. "I appreciate being able to run to the grocery store by myself if I want a Diet Coke, and I don't have to explain why I want it."

Another reason we were good friends: we both liked Diet Coke.

"I had one companion I would classify as my worst. She never talked to me."

"Never? Why did she go on a mission if she didn't like talking to people?"

"That's the thing, she would teach lessons and contact people on the street, but when we were home, she never talked to me."

I looked at her for more of an explanation.

"She would if we were making plans but never about anything personal. It was like she wasn't interested in being friends. At home she would write letters to her family or write in her journal. And she was gross."

I started laughing. "Gross? Do I want to ask why?"

"She would save her dental floss. She laid out a piece of toilet paper on top of the toilet and would put the floss there after she used it. I started keeping track, and she only threw her floss away like every three or four days. And she had really stinky feet. I hoped it was because she wore cheap shoes, but who knows? Maybe that was just her hormonal makeup."

I cringed. "Ew."

"I know. And there was other stuff too."

"Maybe it was better that she wasn't friendly. It made it easier to not like her."

"I did try to like her. Maybe she was a really nice person aside from her gross personal hygiene habits. I tried to be nice and friendly, but she wasn't interested."

"Well, then, she had the problem because you're the nicest girl I know."

"So it was her loss," Gretchen affirmed.

"You'd never hang out at night and talk like what we're doing?"

"Nope."

"Claire, the girl Travis married, was kind of like that. She wasn't really interested in being friends with anyone in the apartment. She lived there, but it seemed like in body only. Everything in her life centered on studying and structure. I wonder how Travis was ever able to start a relationship with her."

"I can't believe he bailed on the marriage. Wow. He was the one who wanted it so bad in the first place."

I pursed my lips. "He was, but I wanted it too." Travis had pushed things fast, but I hadn't exactly told him to slow down.

"Did you have any idea?"

"I was completely blindsided. I mean, once we were married, we argued a lot, but I thought it was normal. It's hard to adjust to living with someone 24/7."

"Yeah, I know. Tell me about it. Some companions I got stuck with would *not* have been my first choice *or* my last choice, for that matter."

We both laughed. Gosh, I had missed her. "I had no idea marriage, or living with Travis, could be so challenging."

"You and I both know Travis could be quite charming." She rolled her eyes.

"He had that act down perfectly. Unfortunately it was just that, an *act*."

"It sounds like it was bad." Gretchen broached the subject gently.

My voice got quiet. "It was bad. I never want to feel that way again. After the divorce, there were days I didn't even get out of bed. I sort of cyberstalked him for a while, bombarding him with e-mails and texts and phone calls for the first couple of weeks. After that I slept and cried all the time. Then I just stayed in bed most of the day, and finally my mom dragged me back to BYU."

Gretchen shook her head in disbelief. "BYU is not the place to be when you have a broken heart."

"I don't even know what Luke saw in me. I was a mess at school. I never got dressed, never did my hair, never put on makeup. I moped around all day and pretended to read books. It was terrible."

"What changed?"

What did change? Where was the turning point? Thanksgiving? Confronting Travis? The Duckk spying day? The change had been impalpable but huge at the same time.

"I don't know exactly. Maybe it was just the passing of time. Maybe it was a bunch of little things that added up to a lot."

As we sat and talked, it was like she had never left.

"I want to know all about this new guy," Gretchen said.

"His name is Luke James." I couldn't stop myself from smiling.

"Do you have pictures? I want to see him."

I pulled out my phone and showed her one from the day he left for Europe. "Oh my gosh. Luke is . . . He's . . . Yeah, I like him." I may have sounded like I was gushing.

"Do you have any more pictures?"

Did I? Like she needed to ask? Like I wasn't going to show her anyway? I started flipping through the pictures.

She examined them. "You really like him. I can tell by the way you say his name." She laughed. "Luuuke," she said dreamily.

I blushed. "Yeah, he's pretty great."

"Great?" she asked, scrolling through the pictures. "Like how great? Like it's great to hang out with him, or he's so great I love him? Are we talking M.M. or E.C.?"

"I love being with him."

Gretchen gave me a sideways look with her eyebrow raised. "Sophia, just admit it. You totally love him."

"No, actually I think I have philophobia." I scratched my neck, suddenly feeling itchy. Maybe I was breaking out in hives.

"Phil-o what? Is that like the cream cheese?" Gretchen squinted at me.

"Philophobia. The fear of falling or being in love. It's been a heated debate between us."

Gretchen giggled. "You think you're afraid of falling in love with him?"

I nodded. "Um, yeah. That about sums it up." I could finally admit what my problem was.

Gretchen started really laughing now.

"What is so funny?" I demanded.

"It's a little too late for that."

I was confused. "What do you mean?"

"You're way past falling in love." She smiled hugely.

Was I?

"The way you're talking and gushing about him, he's totally in the E.C. category."

"No, really." I tried to downplay it. I knew he was E.C. material. But it didn't cancel out my bigger problem. "I'm totally freaked out."

"Why? You say he's a great guy, and you obviously like him. A lot."

"'Cause I made such a big mistake with Travis, and I don't want to do that again."

"But you say Luke's a great guy," Gretchen reiterated.

"He is. And I should know. I've known him longer than I knew Travis, marriage and all."

"I guess experience is the best teacher." She gave me a sympathetic smile. "When does he get back? Isn't it like today or tomorrow?"

"Tomorrow."

"Aren't you excited? You haven't seen him in how long?"

I hesitated.

"What's wrong?"

"I am excited, but things are a little undefined between us right now."

"Undefined? What do you mean?" She waited expectantly for me to fill in the blank.

"He's ready for more, and I just can't . . ." There were so many things I just couldn't do in regards to my relationship with Luke. Because I was afraid.

After a moment of silence, Gretchen changed the subject. "What else have you been doing besides counting the days down until Luke returns?"

"I've been babysitting for my friend Cali part-time. It's been good; it has helped me pass the time until you and Luke got back."

"You babysit?" She was surprised.

"I know. Hard to believe, right? My mother sort of volunteered me slash roped me into doing it for a couple of weeks over last Christmas break. It turned out to be a really good thing. What about you? Are you going to be working? Are you returning to BYU this fall?"

"Hopefully I can find a job this summer, and then I'm going back in the fall."

I had a great idea. "Come live with me. My brother Dan is engaged to my roommate, Rhonda, and she needs to sell her contract. It would be awesome to be roommates again, especially after what I went through with roommates last year. I need you."

"Perfect. I would love that. Then I wouldn't have to find an apartment, and I could live with you. And what's this about your brother?"

"Yes, brother, roommate, getting married in August. She's receiving her endowment in the Salt Lake Temple three days before the wedding, so I'm making a quick trip up to Utah for it, then coming back to Las Vegas for their wedding. Then school starts two weeks later."

"Could I maybe tag along when you go to Utah? I could get my stuff up there early."

"Sure. It will make it more fun. I'll be glad when they're finally married. They're so . . . gushy. By the way, I'm sorry for how disgustingly sappy I must have been with Travis."

"You weren't so bad." Gretchen shook her head.

"Yes, I was. And I am so sorry."

She rolled her eyes. "All right. You were." We both started laughing.

"You seem so different," Gretchen said. I was wondering what she thought it was, because she kept watching me. Not surreptitiously like the girls in my singles ward once the news broke that I was divorced but watching me all the same. "I can't put my finger on it."

"Maybe it's because I've matured like twenty years in the last year."

"Maybe." She shrugged, agreeing, then added, "Not that you were immature before, but I wouldn't say it's all that. It's like you're the same Sophia but different."

"Maybe it's all the substance I've gained." I raised an eyebrow and smiled. "I'm not so shallow anymore."

I think I shocked Gretchen. "Sophia, I wasn't trying to say you were shallow."

This time I shrugged. "*I'm* saying I was." Before Travis, I would have been offended if anyone had suggested I was shallow, let alone claiming it myself. "Things that seemed so important before him and while I was with him don't matter so much to me anymore. I liked it when he spent money on me and bought expensive gifts. But it didn't matter what he bought or how much he spent; he still left me."

"It's still so surprising to me, so incredibly hard for me to believe." Gretchen shook her head slowly.

"That's what I mean about not being so shallow. My life doesn't revolve around shopping and clothes and purses and shoes anymore."

"Well, for the record, I never thought of you as shallow."

"Thanks, Gretch." I smiled. "I'm so glad you're back."

* * *

Gretchen's talk on Sunday was amazing. Even though it was mostly about missionary work, so many things she said related to me.

"I know this might be hard to believe, but I had a hard time deciding if going on a mission was right for me," she began. "I had a lot of doubts. What if I wasn't meant to go on a mission? What if I had to learn a foreign language? What if I wasn't a good missionary? What if I got sent to a foreign country I absolutely didn't want to go to?

"But I took that leap of faith. I made the decision to serve a mission, I went to the Lord in prayer and told Him my decision, and I asked for confirmation. The answer didn't come immediately; it was gradual over the next eighteen months as I served the people of New Zealand, taught them the gospel, and learned to love them as the Lord loved them. I turned my life over to the Lord when I decided to be a missionary, and I have been blessed ever since."

As Gretchen's talk progressed, a couple things she said went right to my heart. I had been self-absorbed lately. I'd been so stuck in my own thoughts and feelings for Luke that little else had mattered. I had justified my behavior at home by feeling entitled to my moodiness. There were worse things in life than having a great boyfriend who loved me. I was being a fence sitter. I needed to get over it and get on with it. I couldn't expect Luke to wait forever. My biggest problem was deciding if I loved Luke. Wow, my perspective was way off.

Now if only I could find the courage to follow through with what I had felt while listening to Gretchen's talk. She made it sound easy. So why was I having such a hard time doing it?

Chapter Fourteen
Visiting Vista

I WIPED MY SWEATY PALMS on my shorts for about the tenth time and tried to ignore the knot in my stomach as I made my way to Luke's house the next day. I had been waiting for this day for weeks, and now that it was finally here, I was filled with trepidation.

I slowly made my way up the street where he lived, looking for his house number. I turned into the driveway, which was long enough that I couldn't see the end. It curved around a tree to reveal a huge house. I wondered if it was a retirement community and maybe his mom had a condo here. I was pretty sure his mom lived alone since Luke's dad had passed away. Maybe I had misunderstood what Luke had told me because this house looked large enough to house a small neighborhood. But he had never made reference to his mother living in a condo. I reviewed anything I could remember him mentioning about where his mother lived. Not much came to mind.

Aside from the surprise of the large house, I was hit by another emotion: worry. I was going to meet his family. His whole family, since they were all going to be there. It was intimidating, especially the thought of meeting his mother. What was it going to be like? Was it going to be like when he met my mother? Was his mom going to be like Maxine? Luke was a kind, gentle person, so he probably had a really nice mom. But thinking back to my experience with my last mother-in-law, I realized I'd thought Travis was an amazing person who had been raised by amazing parents—they had all fooled me. The only thing amazing about them was how amazingly rude they were. I put the car in park and waited for a minute, gathering myself.

Luke's mom opened the front door as I got out of my car. "Sophia," she said with a huge smile, arms wide open. "Hello." She came right up to me and hugged me. Hard. "I'm Kay, Luke's mom."

Kay was the complete opposite of Maxine. I could tell right away, just by her greeting. She was soft compared to Maxine, who was stiff all the way up to her helmet-head hair. Kay was warm and fuzzy inside and out to the point that it was tangible.

"It's nice to meet you," I replied, my cheeks burning. I looked around, waiting for Luke to walk out of the house.

"Well, come on in." Kay grabbed my bag from the trunk of my car. "I'm really excited you could come this weekend."

"Thank you for having me," I said.

I followed her in, looking around to the upstairs landing, still waiting for Luke to come bounding out at any moment. Did he not know I was here? Maybe he was taking a shower. Maybe he wasn't as excited for my visit as I'd hoped.

I was a little in awe as I took in Kay's house/mansion and by the revelation that they were so well off. The money thing had just never come up with Luke. But just because they lived in a big house didn't mean he was rich or, should I say, that his family was. There was a difference, which I'd learned from my last husband.

Kay continued welcoming me as we made our way into the kitchen. "Come in. It is so great to finally meet you." Then she stepped back but held me at arm's length as if to take a good look at me. "Luke has told me everything about you, and I feel like I already know you." She hugged me again.

"Where is Luke?" I wondered out loud, finally having the opportunity to ask. I considered what I should say to Kay, since it was just the two of us and I had never had a one-on-one conversation with her. How long would it be before Luke showed up?

I sat on a barstool at the kitchen island, and Kay chatted cheerfully. "Luke went to the store to buy you some Diet Coke. He said you liked it."

"Oh." I was excited about the Diet Coke but a little disappointed that I didn't get an immediate romantic reunion with him. But maybe it was okay since we also needed to have *that talk*.

"He should be back anytime now." She looked up at the clock. "Would you like a bottle of water while we're waiting?"

I readily agreed, glad to have something to fiddle with. I chewed on my lip, trying to think of what to say. "Luke is a great guy. You must be really proud of him."

I gathered it was the right thing to say from the smile that appeared on her face. "I am very proud of him."

"When I first met him he was, uh . . ." I searched for the right word. *Supportive? Kind? Thoughtful? Understanding? A good friend?* That kind of diminished the whole point of why I'd come here in the first place. "He listened but never pried."

"From what it sounds like, you were quite distraught over your divorce."

"I was a mess back then. It's amazing he even gave me a chance."

Kay patted my hand. "Well, honey, you were grieving. That's a hard thing to go through. And Luke understands grieving, with his dad passing away." I could see where Luke being so easy to talk to came from. Kay was easy to talk to as well.

"When Luke told me about his dad, it gave me hope that things did get better and I could get through it."

"I am a firm believer in the saying 'Time heals all wounds,'" Kay said. "I love Gabe and miss him, but I can still be happy living my life now. I wouldn't miss spending time with my family for anything. Soon after my husband died, I was eating at a Chinese restaurant and my fortune cookie message was, 'Life can only be lived forward but understood backward.' It's silly coming from a fortune cookie, but I needed that advice at the time. I still have the slip of paper. It's a good reminder."

Hadn't I already realized the difference time could make? Hopefully I would get over the baggage from Travis soon. Losing a real husband had to be harder than losing a guy I had only loved for half a year.

She smiled. "Happiness is a choice."

Simply stated like that, yes, it was.

The more I talked with Kay, the more I liked her. I didn't feel inadequate like I had with Maxine. Kay was like the decaffeinated version of my positive mother. She wasn't giving me a pep talk; she was just telling me what she had learned from her experience.

I smiled. "I was lucky to have him as my friend. He probably didn't realize at the time how much his friendship meant to me."

"Well, we think you're great. I know Luke is very happy with you."

I was waiting for the warning. The talk digressing to some sort of *So you better not break his heart.* Or even the warning Maxine had issued about her being the most important woman in her son's life and I had better not try to displace her. But no warning came.

I swallowed hard. "I'm very happy with him." It was the truth, even if things were undecided at the moment.

"Hey, Sophia, you're early," Luke said from behind me.

He was smiling, but I couldn't help but wonder how much of the conversation he had heard, especially the last thing I'd said.

Even with the uncertainty of our relationship, my heart fluttered when I saw him. I hopped up out of the seat so fast I accidentally knocked it over. "Oops," I said, trying to right the chair and hurry over to Luke at the same time. I finally paused to stand the chair up, and Luke came over to me. I gave him a big hug. "I was anxious to see you." Which was true. I was anxious. I wanted things to be settled between us again. I wanted our relationship to go back to being comfortable instead of strained.

I hugged him longer than I should have in front of his mother, enjoying it when he hugged me in return. I stepped back, still unsure what to say or how much affection to show. It was hard to gauge under the circumstances.

"Your mom and I were just . . ." I pointed vaguely to Kay.

"Visiting," Kay filled in. "We were getting to know each other a little. And you were right, Luke; she is gorgeous."

"Mom." Luke was turning a little bit red.

"What exactly have you told her?" I looked at Luke, starting to blush myself. I felt like Kay's comment broke the tension between Luke and me.

"Oh, don't worry, honey. He's just told me enough to know that if he loves you, so do I."

"Mom!"

And the tension suddenly returned. I stiffened a little. Luke hadn't said anything about loving me yet, though I'd had the impression he'd wanted to say it before but hadn't.

I wished I could think of something to say for comic relief, but nothing came to mind.

"How about we bring your bag to your room?" Luke said quickly, picking up my bag.

"Yes, yeah, that would be great," I wanted to leave the awkward situation behind as soon as possible.

"It was nice to meet you," I said to Kay over my shoulder.

"You too, honey." She smiled.

I was surprised when Luke took my hand and led me outside instead of upstairs. "Am I camping?" I joked. I wanted to talk about anything other than what had just happened in the house.

"My mom has you staying in the casita. We thought it'd give you more privacy."

The casita was a minihouse off the main house and close to the pool. It was maybe two hundred fifty square feet and looked like a studio apartment. It had the living room, kitchen, and bedroom all in one room and a bathroom and closet off of that. Very cute.

"This is great," I said, looking around. "I'm surprised there isn't a mint on the pillow." With the bed made and the sheets turned down, I felt like I had stepped into a hotel room.

"Yeah, sorry, no mints."

He came over and finally kissed me properly, making up for his mom's being a part of our six-weeks'-absence reunion. "I've missed you," he said once we broke apart.

I sat down on the bed, and he sat next to me. We were silent for a moment. "I—" I started speaking at the same time Luke did.

"I guess the cat's out of the bag," Luke finally said.

I didn't say anything. I couldn't escape the inevitable discussion. I was hoping he wouldn't bring it up first thing, but then it would be hanging over us until we addressed it, even with how I felt after Gretchen's talk about taking a leap of faith. All my thoughts were in a tangle, and I wasn't sure what exactly I wanted to say. We hadn't said the *L* word yet, and despite feeling very close to him and *maybe* even loving him, I was afraid to go there.

"I'm sorry," Luke said, taking my hand.

"About what? If anyone should be sorry, it's me. I'm sorry for, I don't know, everything." I felt like all this uneasiness in our relationship was my fault. "Dragging my feet, my indecision, my hesitation." Seeing him again, meeting his mom and the rest of the family shortly, and his mother's announcement that he loved me—it was a little too much. I teared up.

"I was just talking about my mom announcing the love thing. She's been really excited to meet you."

I wiped my eyes, embarrassed by my confusion and confession. "Oh, right. I like her. She's very nice."

"Yeah, but I didn't expect her to say something like that."

"Me neither." I opted for comic relief. "I've never had that happen before."

"I hope it didn't freak you out," Luke said softly. "I wanted to tell you at the right time and have it be all romantic."

"Technically your mom said it, which wasn't all that romantic, so you still have your chance."

"Oh, good, then the moment isn't ruined. I wanted to make sure it wasn't going to seem too soon. That's how I planned it. You know, no expectations, no pressure, but just so you know how I feel."

I didn't feel like he was putting pressure on me to figure it out. *I* was putting pressure on myself to have it all figured out and make sure it was right. I liked Luke too much to waste my chance. I hugged him tightly. "Okay," I said.

He kissed my forehead. "What do you want to do? Are you hungry?"

"I was hoping I could get a tour of the house." My plan was to stay busy and hopefully delay *the talk*, although I didn't know how long I could put it off. Wasn't that one of the reasons, even if only in Luke's mind, that I was here? Maybe if I prayed really hard about it tonight, I would be ready to deal with it the next day.

Luke shrugged. "Um, sure, if you want to."

"If I want to? Of course I want to. Your house is beautiful."

"Thanks, I guess. My mom would probably appreciate that compliment more since she's the one who keeps it up."

"Does she take care of the landscaping too? Because you have a really big yard," I said.

"Tell me about it. My dad used to make us mow it every Saturday. Even with a driving lawn mower it took forever."

"I bet."

"My mom takes care of the gardens around the house but has someone come in and do the lawn."

"Yeah," I said, thinking of the meticulously landscaped lawn, "it would take a lot of time."

"The house and yard are getting a little too big for her, I think."

"Why?"

"She's the only one who lives here."

"I was surprised at how big the house was when I drove up. I wasn't sure if it was a little community."

"No, no, this is her house. My dad was a contractor and built it." He said it so casually, like it wasn't this huge spread of a house on a huge spread of land.

Just for the record, it made Travis's parents' house look average.

"It's beautiful and peaceful."

Luke looked out a window. "I think that's one of the reasons my mom doesn't want to move. And the memories."

"Does she have to move?"

He shook his head. "No, but like I said, the house is a little big for just her."

"But when all the family gets together, people need places to stay." Like, for instance, this weekend.

"Yeah. It's hard to leave a place with so many memories."

Once upon a time, it had been hard to leave a place in my mind with certain memories.

"What are you thinking?" He looked at me intently.

"I'm glad I'm not hung up on memories anymore. Why? What are you thinking?"

"I'm thinking how nice it is to be here with you. That I've been wanting and waiting for the right time to tell you I love you."

I considered my response carefully. "I know. I know you love me." My heart started thudding, and I knew this was a chance to take that leap of faith in our relationship.

"You do?"

"Yes. Remember? Your mom told me." I tried not to smile, but it snuck across my face.

"Dang." He grinned. "I need to tell her to stop doing that."

Making light of it worked this time, but I knew I couldn't avoid saying it forever.

"You ready?" He nodded toward the door.

"I'll be out in a minute. I want to brush my teeth and change. I smell like the nasty truck stop I stopped at on the way down."

"Then I'll let you have your privacy, and I'll see you out there."

I cleaned up as quickly as I could, and when I came out, Luke was sitting on a patio chair, waiting for me.

He took my hand and led me into the house to start the grand tour, which was pretty grand. The house included six bedrooms, a formal living room, a formal dining room, an upstairs family room, a downstairs family room, a kitchen, a loft that doubled as a playroom for the grandkids, and a theater downstairs.

"Awesome," I said as I walked into the theater and looked around. There were two huge sectional sofas around the perimeter of the room. "Do you guys hang out in here a lot?"

Luke scrunched his face. "Not so much now. When we were younger, we did."

I sat down on one of the sofas. "These sofas are way more comfortable than actual theater chairs." I leaned back.

Luke settled in next to me. "People have been known to fall asleep in these."

"Probably not the best idea for us to take a nap," I said. "I don't want your mom to come looking for us, thinking we might be making out or something."

He chuckled. "Yeah, we wouldn't want that to happen." He stood and pulled me up with him. My hand slipped into his familiar grasp, and we went upstairs.

* * *

"Is your whole family here already?" I whispered to Luke when I heard voices upstairs.

"Not yet, but they are all coming today. Sounds like Matt and Steph are here."

"Do you think your family is going to like me?"

I hoped his answer wouldn't be something like "I don't need their approval" or "It doesn't matter what they think." I had learned with Travis that family was a big influence on a relationship and marriage.

Luke squeezed me. "They are going to love you."

"Do you really think so?"

"Of course they will." He glanced over his shoulder. "Hey, Matt. Hey, Steph. You guys made it."

"Luke." His oldest brother set down a duffel bag and walked over and hugged him. You could tell they were brothers—they had the same dark hair, full lips, and smooth voice. Steph joined in, carrying a sleepy child in her arms.

"Hi, Luke." She turned and smiled at me. "You must be Sophia."

"Yes, nice to meet you," I said, hanging back beside Luke.

His brother shook my hand, and his sister-in-law gave me a hug despite the sleeping child. "It's nice to meet you," Steph said.

As she headed into the house, a little girl ran up to me, blonde curls bouncing. "I'm Lindy. I'm five."

I squatted down so I was eye level with her. "Nice to meet you, Lindy."

"Are you Uncle Luke's friend?"

"Yes." I nodded my head.

Her eyebrows raised. "His *special* friend?"

"Sure, I guess you could say that." I agreed and smiled at her. Five-year-olds were so cute.

"Like his girlfriend?"

I nodded my head.

"Do you guys kiss?" She twisted up her face. Apparently she thought kissing was gross.

I laughed at her expression. "Sometimes."

"Are you going to get married?"

I hadn't expected that question, but coming from a five-year-old, I shouldn't have been surprised. "I don't know. We'll have to wait and see."

"Maybe next week?" she said hopefully.

"Lindy," her dad warned.

I shook my head. "Probably not."

"Then how about the next week after that?"

"Nothing has been planned."

"Can I be in your wedding? Please, please, please? My best friend got to be in one, and she wore a princess dress and got her nails painted."

I smiled at Lindy. She really didn't want to know the state of our relationship so much as to reserve her claim as flower girl. "Tell you what, honey, as soon as I know anything, I'll let you know. Okay?"

She seemed satisfied with that, gave me a spontaneous hug, and ran off into the house, most likely to tell her mother the good, but unsubstantiated, news.

Was the assumption made that bringing someone home equaled marrying them? That was exactly what had happened when Luke visited my family, and we hadn't even dated yet. Even little Lindy knew there was a difference between a friend and a *special* friend.

Chapter Fifteen
Nervous, to Say the Least

"Nothing like throwing me into the fire and making me meet everyone all at once," I said to Luke as I jabbed him in the ribs with my elbow. We were returning from a movie, part of my plan to stay busy, and from the number of cars in the driveway, I knew the others had arrived.

"It's my way of getting you back for when I met your family." He smiled, then took my hand and led me into the house.

"Hey, it was your idea to visit," I reminded him.

"So this can't be any worse."

"Nothing could be worse. Unless your mother or brothers ask me what my intentions are with you." Then I laughed, partly because of the embarrassment that still lingered from the first time Luke had met my family. "Does your family snort, by chance?"

"Not at the dinner table."

"I'll try to make sure I don't, then," I said.

"That might be a good idea."

As I took in the group gathered in the kitchen, Luke gave me a rundown on who was who and a little bit of background on each of them.

"Matt is the one you met earlier, and his wife is obviously Stephanie. Everyone calls her Steph. They have four children: Chase, Madison, Lindy, and Jaxon. Steph stays at home, and Matt works as a data analyst, whatever that means. She likes to bake cookies. She's really nice and funny."

"Funnier than me?"

"No one makes me laugh like you do." He grinned at me.

"Okay, Matt and Steph," I repeated back. "Chase, Madison, Lindy, and Jaxon."

"Mark is married to April. He's in medical equipment sales, and April stays at home but does photography. It's like a hobby/side business. They have two children: Brooklyn and Katelyn. She homeschools them, does natural childbirth, and feeds them only organic food. It seems like a lot of work to me. At least she's nice and doesn't really push her point of view. Just don't get into a discussion about the evils of immunizations."

"I won't tell her I'm immunized," I whispered.

Luke started laughing.

"And I won't even touch her opinion about doing childbirth without drugs."

"I have to agree with you on that one. I don't want to be disabled by you squeezing my hand too hard." Luke laughed, then suddenly stopped.

There was a pregnant pause. Or just a very, very awkward one.

I swallowed and ignored it. "Anything else I need to know? Or know to avoid?"

"She likes to stay on schedule. Like, guaranteed she leaves the dinner table tonight, no matter what's going on, to put the kids to bed at their bedtime."

"Mark and April. April's all-natural."

Luke continued. "Leia is married to Mike. They have two kids: Emily and Micah. Leia spends any spare time scrapbooking or making crafts. She's very cool, especially for a sister."

"Okay. Scrappy and craftsy."

"And finally there's John and Kimmy. Never make the mistake of calling her Kim. She hates that. They've been married two years, no kids. John is applying to dental school, and Kimmy has her own catering business."

"Kim, not Kimmy. Caterer."

"No, it's Kimmy, not Kim. You got it backwards."

"Right, Kimmy, not Kim," I repeated back.

"She's only touchy when it comes to her name and food. Other than that, she's nice. But they are bringing their little dog, Einstein. Is that a problem? Didn't you say you were allergic to them?"

"Maybe. What is it?

"A miniature poodle."

"I think those are hypoallergenic. I should be okay. If not, I'll take some Benadryl and possibly fall asleep in my dinner plate." I was at least hopeful the dog wouldn't make me sneeze.

"Yeah, I don't know how they'd react if we asked them to keep the dog outside. He's sort of like their kid."

"They don't feed it food with their mouths, do they?"

"What?" He blinked, confused.

"Didn't I ever tell you about that girl in our ward who asked my advice about getting married right after news of my divorce broke?"

"I don't think so."

I shook my head, still awed by what she told me. "She said she loved her boyfriend but thought his parents were weird. They fed the dog food from their mouths."

"Like, already-been-chewed?"

"No, I think they would put the food between their teeth for the dog to take."

Luke scowled. "Sounds gross."

I nodded. "I know."

"I'm pretty sure John and Kimmy don't feed the dog that way. At least I've never seen it."

"Let's hope not."

"Besides, Kimmy's very particular about what food the dog eats. He's on a special diet, or she thinks he needs to lose weight, or he can only eat a certain type of food. I don't remember exactly, but she's very strict about it."

I leaned in close to him. "Okay, I won't feed the dog table food, and I'll stay clear when she's in the kitchen. She'd probably consider what we did to that turkey we cooked animal cruelty."

Luke gave me a squeeze. "Probably a good idea if we both stay out of the kitchen when it comes to Thanksgiving preparations."

"We'll just invite ourselves to her house for Thanksgiving," I suggested.

"That sounds like the best option."

"At least a safe option."

With the CliffsNotes version of family members, I was plunged into the world of the James family.

As we came in, Steph walked over. "Hey, guys. You're back just in time to eat."

"We planned it that way," Luke said with feigned innocence.

"Do you two mind helping set the table and carrying the food out?" She motioned with her head toward the back patio.

"Sure," Luke and I both said.

I followed Luke and Steph into the kitchen, where there was an impressive-looking spread of food on the island, never mind the incredible aroma of whatever was cooking.

Kimmy, dressed with a white apron, was in the midst of the preparations, looking serious and in charge. The impression I had from Luke's description was that she was all business, which was an apt description. She was only about five feet tall, tiny, maybe a hundred pounds. Thick dark hair cut in a short bob hung just below her ears. All her moves were exact and precise. She seemed intimidating.

The person who I assumed by deduction was April was also helping out in the kitchen. She looked up and smiled and gave a small wave. She didn't go natural when it came to her looks. She was obviously meticulous, her high ponytail perfectly smooth and shiny, her makeup flawless, her outfit trendy.

Steph pointed out what needed to be done. "There's the tablecloths and tableware. Let's have you do that first, and then we'll bring the food out. Thanks, guys."

I wasn't completely comfortable just yet, but I was much more comfortable here than I'd ever felt in Maxine's kitchen.

Luke and I carried the stuff outside and set it on two long picnic tables. I was reminded of a scene out of the pages of *Better Homes and Gardens*. The patio covering was lined with strings of lights, the table looked festive, the food smelled delicious, the family seemed happy, and we were poolside. Rhonda would have been very impressed with the presentation.

When we went back inside, Kay asked me to finish mixing the potato salad, which only needed mayonnaise and mustard. I did as I was told, hoping there was no way I could screw it up. Once it was all mixed, I covered it and brought it out to the table.

When I walked back in the kitchen, Luke was talking with Mark. I saw him before he saw me, and a feeling of affection washed over me.

This sudden flow of emotion took me by surprise, and I stopped midstep to consider my crazy thoughts. Luke looked over at precisely the same moment, and a wide smile broke out on his face. I realized how happy I was to be there.

* * *

"Tell us about yourself," Matt said once we were all seated for dinner and formal introductions had been made. Luke's siblings were all named after the books of the New Testament, except Leia, so it made it really easy to remember them. I just had to make sure I put the right name to the right face. The wives' and children's names were still a little sketchy. Once they were all seated by their husbands, it was easier to figure out who was who.

"Well, I'm . . ." I hesitated because I almost said divorced. But then I remembered the whole redefine thing and decided to say something different. "So, I, uh . . . I'm from Vegas. I'm nineteen."

"How'd you meet Luke?" Leia eagerly asked.

"At BYU. He was my home teacher."

"Bet you hated that assignment, huh, Luke?" Mark ribbed him.

I blushed a little.

"I'm sorry. I don't mean to embarrass you. It's more to embarrass Luke," Mark said, then smiled. "He's never brought a girl home before."

I swallowed. "I know."

"Thanks, Mark," Luke said.

"That's how you two met?" April said. "Luke was your home teacher?"

I nodded.

Luke took over the explanation. "Sophia was quite elusive. Everyone was asking her out, but no one was successful." That was a nice way of putting it: elusive. He could have said depressed, a train wreck, or so many other things to describe what I was when I'd first met him.

Leia laughed. "How'd you manage to succeed?"

"My good looks and charm and the fact that I was named after Luke Skywalker," Luke joked, and his siblings busted out laughing.

"Okay, you met at BYU, at church. What happened next?" Steph prompted.

"Um." I looked at Luke. "We . . ." So many details; which ones to edit?

"Met up in the laundry room one night, both trying to avoid the ward talent show. Sophia liked to hide out there."

"Laundry was my excuse to protect me from my overzealous roommate who was like a one-woman social committee." I didn't want them to think I was a crazy girl who liked hanging out in dingy laundry rooms.

"Who is now becoming her sister-in-law," Luke said, chuckling.

"Oh no," Steph said.

"Oh, yes." I rolled my eyes. "I'm so looking forward to it."

Everyone started laughing.

"So . . . ?" Kimmy pressed.

I was surprised she was interested. But here at the table, away from the kitchen, she seemed a little softer.

I figured it was better to get it out of the way at first. It made it easier to get on to normal topics of conversation. "I was still having a hard time with my divorce and was kind of antisocial."

"Luke told us. It sounded like it was difficult," April said.

"Luke convinced me to come over for Thanksgiving, and we had a pretty bad experience with the turkey."

"Like what?" John asked.

"We, uh . . ." Luke hedged, "sort of burned the outside of the turkey and didn't cook the inside."

"You let Luke cook?" Kimmy looked at me like I was nuts.

To which Luke grinned. "Yeah, I cooked. The only time Sophia cooked a turkey, she sent three people to the emergency room with food poisoning."

Almost everyone gasped in unison.

I crinkled my nose, hating to admit it, and nodded my head.

"You've got to tell us what happened," Kay said.

I shook my head. "It was bad. Really bad." They all waited for me to tell the story. "Well, it was right before I got married. Somehow my future mother-in-law dumped the turkey responsibility on me. I was only eighteen; I had never cooked a turkey before. So I cooked it as best I could. Long story short, it was taking too long, and we needed to get to their house, so I took it out of the oven before it was done. Then everyone ended up with food poisoning."

"Turkeys can be intimidating." Kimmy patted my hand. Again, I was surprised at her show of kindness.

"It was awkward poisoning my future in-laws two days before the wedding. Then the doctor suggested I pick up some adult diapers, and, yeah, it was bad. Very, very embarrassing. I've vowed to stay away from turkeys."

"Talking about embarrassing," Kay said, "today at the drive thru, the person at the payment window looked at me really weird when I paid. I didn't know why, so I was just friendly and smiled. Then the girl at the food window gave me a really strange look. I wasn't sure what was going on until I looked in the rearview mirror and saw one of the lenses of my sun glasses had fallen out. But it was on my lazy-eye side, and I can't see out of that one very well anyway, so I had no idea I was driving around looking like a fool." Then she clapped her hands and started laughing at herself.

Everyone joined in. Maxine would have never laughed about that. She was always so formal and proper. So uptight.

"I think I can top that," Leia said. "I've been up so much with the baby at night because of her ear infections that I look tired all the time. My girlfriend suggested Preparation H because it helps reduce swelling . . . under my eyes, I mean." Everyone laughed. "I found out, going through airport security, that Preparation H is not an approved carry-on item, or maybe my tube was just too big, because it was confiscated. But not before the security checked loudly with the other security guards whether or not my ointment could go through."

"Does it really work?" I blurted out, curious. It sounded crazy to me. "I could have used that tidbit of knowledge back at school when crying was a regularly scheduled activity. Maybe Luke wouldn't have worried so much about me, being my home teacher and all. He always seemed to catch me at my worst and still acknowledged he knew me."

"Luke has always been a gentleman." Steph smiled at him.

"Yeah, he's come to my rescue more than once," I said, thinking about the Big Date fiasco. I changed the subject back to cooking.

"I do have to say it was nice to be invited into the kitchen to help with the food tonight. I was kind of banished by my in-laws after the turkey-poisoning incident."

"That was before we knew your track record," Kimmy said, winking at me.

"I think we've all had our share of embarrassing moments. I think one of the greatest gifts we can give ourselves in life is the ability to laugh at ourselves. Life can be very funny if we see the humor in things," Steph said.

"Amen," her husband added.

Leia leaned in close. "You can tell me if I'm being too nosy, but is there a wedding in the future?" she asked quietly.

"Just my brother's," I answered.

Chapter Sixteen
Challenged

WHEN ALL WAS SAID AND done, the dishes stacked, the table cleared, the food put away, we went back inside to the family room for what Kay called "game time." It sounded fun until I found out it was Wii games. Board games, I was fine with. The Wii, well, let's just say coordination was not my best asset. Put a Wii remote in my hand, and everyone had better steer clear. It had happened not once, not twice, but three times that I had injured someone with a whack to the head or the arm or thrown the remote into the air. I was Wii challenged.

Most of the games we played were team sports, the teams being the couples. But there were a few individual games. I won the bowling, thanks to the BYU bowling class I'd taken. I was relieved I'd made it through without any flying remotes or injuries, but as I was celebrating my bowling victory, I took a step back and accidentally stepped on the dog, who was somehow sleeping soundly at the edge of the couch. The dog yelped and jumped up, throwing me off balance and making me stumble into the kitchen island. I reached out to steady myself but instead hit a bowl of fruit dip, sending it flying onto the floor.

Fortunately the bowl was plastic. Unfortunately it landed upside down, dumping the contents all over the floor. The dog, frightened by the noise, ran in circles, then straight at the bowl, knocking into it and sending it skidding across the floor. The dog started licking the Marshmallow-Kreme and cream-cheese dip—not that we could have saved it, since it was on the floor, but now it was definitely inedible.

"Stop! The dog can't eat that! He'll get sick," Kimmy yelled.

Steph's baby crawled over to it as if he knew it was something he wasn't supposed to get into. Before anyone could grab him, he had both hands covered in the mixture and in his mouth. Apparently it was so good he dropped onto his tummy and started licking the floor alongside the dog.

"Jaxon, no!" Steph hurried over to him.

Kimmy clapped. "Einstein. Einstein. No. Stop it!"

For a dog named after a brilliant man, he was either a genius for realizing what he was eating was a no-no or was named wrong because he was dumb enough to eat anything that happened to fall on the floor. I couldn't decide which.

Chaos ensued as Steph and Kimmy scrambled toward their babies. Leia jumped up and rushed to the kitchen in search of paper towels, and the kids gathered around to check out the carnage. It wasn't my finest moment, by any means, but it was more like a scene the true Sophia would display.

April appeared behind me. "That was an easy way to get rid of that dip. Probably a good thing since I could have single-handedly eaten all of it myself."

Somehow I doubted that, considering how Luke had told me she was super healthy. "It was really good," I murmured, standing there watching the disaster I had created unfold.

"That was awesome, Dad!" Matt's oldest son, Chase, said. "Did you see how that bowl went flying in the air?"

Who didn't see it? I thought self-consciously.

"Chase." Matt guided him to sit next to him before he said something to him in a quiet voice I couldn't hear. I'm sure it was something to do with being considerate about the situation.

Leia's son Micah was just as excited as Chase. "Yeah! Cool!" He was jumping up and down and cheering.

"Micah!" Leia said sternly. "Calm down. You're making the dog more excited."

I was waiting for Mark and April's kids to get in on it, but their two girls just stood and stared, eyes bulging. Perhaps this kind of chaos never happened at their house.

"John, do you think Einstein will be okay?" Kimmy was freaking out about how much dip the dog had ingested.

Kay came over to me. "Don't worry, Sophia. I made a double batch."

It wasn't the fruit dip I was worried about. It was more my bruised ego and the embarrassing and probably lasting impression I had just made on the family.

Luke came up behind me and put his hand on the small of my back. "You okay? You have this look of . . ."

"Total humiliation?" I filled in for him. The words caught in my throat.

"No. Oh, hey, don't cry." Luke's voice was soothing.

I tried to look away before he saw the tears lining my eyes, but he knew me too well.

"You want to go outside for a minute?"

"I should help clean up." I looked at the scene, feeling helpless.

Luke looked in the same direction. "They've got it handled," he said, nudging me toward the backyard.

Going outside and getting away from the excitement was a welcome suggestion. I needed some fresh air. Once outside I took a deep breath and wiped my eyes.

"I know you don't think so, but it was hilarious," Luke said, sitting down at the edge of the pool.

"Yeah," I said, sitting next to him and putting my feet in the pool. "Great impression I'm making. Everyone will reminisce about the time I killed Kimmy's dog."

Luke chuckled. "I don't think Einstein's going to die. It was probably his best day ever because he got to eat forbidden food. Look at it like you were doing the dog a favor. He might be deprived for the rest of his dog life."

"You can't take me anywhere," I said.

He bumped me with his shoulder. "Oh, please, honey. Your clumsiness is part of the reason I love you."

"It is? Really? Why?" I challenged him.

"It keeps you humble," he said with a completely straight face.

I swatted at him. "You're joking."

He cracked up laughing "I am. But it's true. Your clumsiness is very endearing. It gives me a chance to rescue you."

"Luke, if you haven't noticed, we tend to be clumsy together. Remember when I spilled the slushie at the store, and we both slipped in it?"

"Touché. Point taken. But I do find you endearing."

I rolled my eyes and patted his chest. "I'm glad you consider it endearing and not embarrassing."

"You could never embarrass me."

"You say that now. Don't be too sure. We've had the turkey incident, the slushie incident, meeting my family and all of them laughing and snorting while eating lunch, and knocking over fruit dip tonight. The list is only going to get longer, and I'm eventually going to embarrass you."

"I'll take my chances," he said as he leaned in to kiss me.

"Hey, guys. You out here?" Leia called out.

"Yeah, we're just . . ." Luke started.

She walked over and sat down next to us.

"Just trying to recover from total humiliation." I smiled, deciding that making light of it was better than feeling sorry for myself.

"Well, don't feel too humiliated. Micah just barfed all over the carpet. Mike is cleaning it up because the smell is making me want to throw up."

"Dang!" Luke said with mock disappointment. "I was just going to offer to go in there and cause a diversion, like breaking a window with the Wii remote or throwing up on the living room floor or . . ."

I giggled and leaned into him. "You'd do that for me?"

"Of course. If Leia's kid hadn't stolen my idea."

Leia shook her head. "Never a dull moment when kids are involved."

"Or me," I added. "This will be remembered as the night Sophia killed Einstein." I sighed.

Leia started laughing. "Don't worry. That dog loved it. Did you see Kimmy's face?" Leia did an impersonation. "Einstein! Einstein!" Leia started waving her arms frantically, her voice way shriller than Kimmy's had been. "Don't eat that!"

Her impersonation was dead-on and hilarious. "Besides, game night was starting to get boring. It usually ends with the kids having meltdowns because they didn't win and they're overtired or something awful. You saved us from the kids turning on each other, brother on brother, sister-in-law on sister-in-law. It can get ugly."

"Really?" I couldn't imagine that; everyone seemed to get along so well.

"No, not really, but it was getting time for April to put her kids to bed." Leia gave me a look of confirmation. "Are you guys coming back in?" She stood up.

"Yeah, we'll come back in soon," Luke said.

I mustered up a smile and nodded at Leia.

Luke helped me up. He didn't say anything but kissed me on the forehead before we went back in to join the others. I was planning on taking a bow, saying that was all the entertainment for this evening, and mentioning there might be more to come tomorrow, but no one even noticed our return. I was relieved to see that things had moved past my embarrassing moment. Most of the kids were in the process of being wrangled up the stairs to be put to bed, and Matt invited us to watch a movie after in the theater with the rest of Luke's siblings. Nothing more was said about my clumsiness. And best of all, Einstein was still alive and well.

As I sat there, I had a weird feeling. I was comfortable despite my clumsiness. I fit right in, felt right at home, even if I'd dumped the dip. Everyone was friendly and welcoming. Even Kimmy. To sum it up, I felt like I was a part of their family. And it totally freaked me out.

When the movie ended, Luke accompanied me upstairs and outside. I thought he was walking me to the casita, but instead he led me over to the patio chairs, where we sat down.

"It's so beautiful tonight," I said quietly, reaching for his hand. "The lights reflecting off of the pool, the full moon, the warm breeze. I could get used to living like this."

Luke was quiet for several moments before he finally spoke. "Where do you see this going?" he asked.

His bluntness surprised me. "As in us?"

"Yeah, us."

I certainly hadn't seen that question coming right now. We were having *the talk*. I stiffened a little. I hated defining our relationship any more than what we already had. Wasn't that good enough for now? I loved being with him; we had a good time together. Admitting my feelings for him and actually saying them out loud scared me. I didn't want things to move too fast, like they had with Travis. I needed to wait just a little longer. I had to be absolutely sure this time around. No doubts.

I let go of his hand and swung my legs around so I was facing him. "Um, I don't know," I answered weakly. Even though I remembered everything I had thought and felt at Gretchen's homecoming, I couldn't take that leap.

"You know I love you, Sophia."

"I know. Isn't that enough for now?"

His voice got an ever-so-slight edge to it. Even in the moonlight, I could see a muscle in his jaw tense. "I'm thinking more long-term."

He was thinking marriage. I knew that. It was one of the things that petrified me the most. Because what if it all fell apart again?

I rubbed my forehead before looking at him. "It's hard for me because of what happened—"

"I'm not Travis. You should know that by now. I don't treat you like he did—"

"I know you're not Travis. It's just that . . ."

"What?" Luke demanded before I could even finish.

This was turning into a fight of unfinished thoughts and sentence fragments. "It's nothing to do with you," I blurted out. "It's me."

"You're kidding. The 'It's not you; it's me' line? That's the oldest excuse in the book." He sounded exasperated.

"What if I'm wrong again?" The words tumbled out before I could stop them. My mouth fell open, and I was horrified that I'd said it out loud.

"Does it feel wrong?" He looked at me.

"No." But I hadn't thought it felt wrong with Travis either. Only I couldn't tell Luke that.

"Then it shouldn't be a problem," he said slowly.

"Please don't do this right now," I begged.

"Do what? I just want to know if you love me."

"You know how much I care about you. Can't we just enjoy being together for a while without rushing into marriage?"

"It's been six months. Six months is not rushing." His words were measured and even.

Everything started feeling tight around me. My heart pounded, and my throat constricted. "Don't push me."

"I'm not pushing you." He rubbed his neck and stared at the ground. Was he too exasperated to look at me?

"Well, maybe I just can't make that kind of commitment right now."

He looked at me and narrowed his eyes. "You remember how you told me you were willing to do whatever it took to work things out with Travis and he wasn't willing to work at it?" he said quietly.

"That has nothing to do with this."

"Yeah, well, who's acting like Travis now?" he said, getting up from his chair and walking away.

How dare he accuse me of acting like Travis! I *was* trying. I was just anxious. Very, very anxious. "I'm not acting like Travis!" I yelled at his back.

Luke didn't stop or even turn around to look at me. "It's called emotional investment. Maybe you should try it," he yelled back before he went into the house and slammed the door behind him.

I waited for him to return. After about fifteen minutes, I gave up. I guess that was good night.

Which made for a really bad night.

Chapter Seventeen

Preparation H for Soothing Relief

I NEEDED PREPARATION H. MY eyes were puffy—a telltale sign of the emotional night I'd had. I'd finally cried myself to sleep, only to toss and turn the rest of the night.

I blamed Travis for my emotional hang-ups. It was all his fault. But in the end, I needed to pull on my big-girl pants and take responsibility for my feelings. But doing that did nothing for my eyes. I snuck out, tiptoeing around the side of the house, and hopped in the car. I stopped at the first store I found, hoping it carried Preparation H. I thought 7-Eleven should have something like that, right? I'd probably pay double what it was at Target, but I was desperate. I needed a miracle.

Sure enough, there was a tiny tube in their tiny toiletry section with a not-so-tiny price. I justified the cost by reminding myself I was desperate. I couldn't face Luke and his family at breakfast with eyes looking like this. I also grabbed a small bottle of Visine. It had been my best friend during my divorce-recovery days, and I hoped it would do the trick again this morning.

As I pulled up to the house, I could see movement through the window, which probably meant breakfast was starting. Great. I was hoping everyone would sleep in and I could slip back into the casita unnoticed, take care of my traitor eyes, and make some sort of attempt to pretend everything was normal with me at breakfast. It looked like it wasn't going to happen, especially since they were serving breakfast on the patio. Dang it.

Using the rearview mirror to apply the cream in the car became my backup plan. I ripped open the box and squeezed a little of the cream onto my index finger, then smeared it under both eyes. I didn't think I could safely put it on my eyelids without getting it in my eyes, which would cause a whole new set of problems. I wondered how long it would take to see results. Come to find out, not long at all.

And something was very wrong. Something was burning. That was not a good sign.

Menthol. Vapors. Had I bought mentholated? I grabbed the box, blinking back the tears. Sure enough, I'd bought the wrong kind. Great. How did I miss that little detail? I searched in the car for a napkin and found one wadded up in the bottom of the console. It was a little dusty, but I didn't care. I needed that cream off now.

It didn't take more than a few seconds to realize that just wiping it wasn't going to do the job. I needed soap. What in the world had I been thinking, putting a cream made for a very different reason anywhere near my eyes? Talk about a momentary lapse of reasoning.

I skipped the Visine, figuring the Preparation H would cancel out the purpose of eye drops. I hid the cream at the bottom of my purse and went to the gate at the side of the house. Hopefully no one would see me slipping back into the casita and I could take care of my little problem.

But the gate was locked.

I kicked myself for not thinking to use a rock to prop it open. The only way in now was through the house.

I tried to be as quiet as possible as I closed the front door, reminding myself to be grateful the front door was unlocked; otherwise, I would have had to ring the bell.

"Good morning, Sophia," Kay said before she looked up from where she was sitting in the family room. "Oh, honey. Is something wrong? You're crying."

"It's Preparation H," I explained, blinking back the tears. "I bought the wrong kind."

Kay let out a little laugh. "Oh my. Do you need to wash your face?"

I nodded. "I think I better." I blinked double speed, trying to stop the burning.

Kay took hold of my arm and gently led me up the stairs to her bathroom. "Here's some face cleaner and a washcloth and towel." She set it all down next to me. "I'll go find an elastic to pull your hair up. I'll be right back." She patted me on the back and left me to my attempt to remove any residue of the cream.

I washed and rewashed the area until I thought I'd be okay.

"Here you go." She joined me in the bathroom again. "Is it better now?"

I blinked a few times, testing to see if there was any burning left. "I think so." I looked up at where she was sitting on the edge of her deep, massive tub.

It was quiet for a moment, and I felt the need to offer some sort of explanation, even though Kay had yet to ask. I could see where Luke had learned not to pry.

"I didn't sleep well," I said.

"I hope it wasn't because of the sleeper sofa. I never sleep on it and worry about how comfortable it is."

"Actually, no, the mattress felt really nice, thank you."

"Oh, don't thank me. It was Luke." She smiled. "He insisted on buying a memory-foam mattress topper before you came."

"Luke," I said, feeling worse and worse.

"Yes, he took care of making up the bed and everything."

I was having a helping of humble pie for breakfast.

"Do you have a lot on your mind?" Kay asked gently.

"Yeah, I do." I shrugged, trying to be nonchalant. "And I thought I'd try Leia's suggestion of using Preparation H for bags under your eyes, but it obviously went horribly wrong."

"I remember what it was like being young and in love. I would go to great lengths to impress Gabe."

I didn't want to tell her I wasn't trying to impress Luke. She didn't need to know I was going to such great lengths to conceal the truth that I had been crying all night.

"I better go check on breakfast. I'll see you in a few minutes."

"Thanks," I said, then looked at my reflection in the mirror. After all the washing and rubbing, my eyes were red and blotchy. I'm sure there was a cream for that sort of problem, but I wasn't in the mood to try any more.

After a few minutes of applying a cold washcloth, wishing I had some cucumber slices handy, and a few more minutes to calm down, I peeked around the bathroom door. I didn't see anyone, and I held on to the hope that I could sneak back to the casita so no one would have to witness my debacle.

I made it outside successfully and did what I could to repair the damage, then I went to face my fate. Breakfast was a little strenuous. For Luke and me, at least. Everyone around us was talking and making plans for the day. Luke and I sat there, not joining in on the conversation and not interacting with each other. I tried to choke down half a bagel but finally gave up, stood up, threw my barely eaten bagel away, took my Diet Coke, and feebly excused myself. Luke followed me as I headed to the casita, and he softly shut the door behind him once we were in. He tentatively sat on the edge of the bed.

"What's wrong with your eyes? Did Einstein get to you?"

Normally I would have found his comment funny, but today, not so much. "It's nothing," I said flatly.

And then there was silence.

Deafening silence.

Luke finally broke it. "Sorry about last night. I didn't mean to be so demanding."

I choked up a little. He had nothing to apologize for. It was all me. I sat next to him, and my eyes began tearing up. This time it had nothing to do with Preparation H. "Maybe we should start over." I forced a smile.

"Good idea."

"I'm sorry about last night. I couldn't stop thinking," I began. I wanted to add that I was completely overanalyzing everything, including my feelings for him. Everything had seemed so perfect last night—being with him, being with his family, telling the story about how we'd started dating. Then he'd asked that one question that had changed everything, and I was freaked out. Why did I have to be so freaked out? Maybe because I had thought everything was so perfect with Travis and it really hadn't been. Was I just doing the same thing over again? Maybe I was waiting for the other shoe to drop. Was I convincing myself that whomever I was with was the perfect guy? Or that this was too perfect?

"Hey." Luke brought me out of my thoughts.

He bent down, trying to catch my eye, so I faked a smile and cleared my throat. "I thought we were at a good place." I didn't want to harp on it, but it felt unsettled. Unsettled things had a way of multiplying when left to my own thoughts.

Luke shrugged. "We are at a good place. But seeing you last night made me realize some things. Maybe I should explain where I was coming from."

"Like what?"

"It's easy for a person to act one way when you're alone with them but another way when they're surrounded by others."

I furrowed my brows. "I don't know if I'm following."

"It was nice to see you with my family last night. Everyone likes you. You fit right in. You seem pretty comfortable with them."

I was still trying to follow how fitting in with his family brought on the fight last night. I thought it was just about my being able to say "I love you" to him.

Oh. Wait. Figured it out. Freaked me out. More.

Luke continued. "My mom really likes you. She wishes she had more time to visit with you. She feels like you're part of the family."

There it was again, fitting right into the family. Why did Luke keep bringing that up? My heart was pounding; my thoughts were racing. I felt a little claustrophobic. Should I take what he said at face value or read into it? "Can we talk about something else?" I mumbled. "I'm freaking out just a little."

I wanted to take the words back as soon as they came out. A hurt look crossed Luke's face.

"Why?" he sounded confused.

I should have thought of a better way to express myself. "I don't know."

"What exactly freaks you out? That I like that you fit in with my family? Or I'm happy because it feels like you belong? Is that so bad?"

"No. I like your family," I said. "It's just . . ."

"What?" He didn't demand it, but he didn't exactly ask gently.

"I'm afraid to go *there*."

"Where exactly is *there*?"

"You know . . . *there*." I was frustrated, and my throat was tight. He knew what I was talking about. This was turning into a mess again.

"No, Sophia, I'm not exactly sure where *there* is." His words were curt. "All I know is how I feel for you. And I think you feel the same, but you won't talk about it." The edge from last night crept back into Luke's voice.

"I wish I could go back to being happy and trusting so blindly." I sighed, hating what I was about to admit.

Luke's eyebrows knitted together. "You're not happy?"

"I am happy. It's just that . . ."

"What?" Luke waited.

"I wish Travis hadn't ruined everything for me." If it hadn't been for him, my relationship with Luke would be different. I wouldn't be so hesitant. I could naively believe that being in love was enough to make a marriage last.

Luke took a deep breath. "Why does Travis always come up?"

"Because my baggage has his name on it." I suggested it as a joke, but by the scowl on Luke's face, I could tell he didn't find me amusing. I hated the truth, but that was it.

"Honey, how are we ever going to move forward if you're still hanging on to that baggage?"

"It's not like I can just let it go," I said.

"I don't get it. I thought you made your peace with him."

"You don't understand—"

"Then *make* me understand. Make me understand why we're even talking about Travis." He let out a huff and shook his head. His lips twitched momentarily as if he wanted to say something more but was stopping himself.

"You know what? Let's just not even talk about it," I said.

Luke rested his head in his hand. "We're going to have to talk about it sometime."

"Why?"

"Because ignoring it is not making it go away. Travis somehow creeps into almost every conversation—never mind into our relationship. I'm beginning to think I'm dating him too."

I didn't say anything because I knew he was right.

"And I can't even tell you how I feel without you getting upset and defensive and avoiding the topic."

"I'm sorry. I'm trying; it's just not easy."

Luke ran his hand through his hair, then rubbed his temples like he had a headache. "Maybe you need to get this figured out. I'm tired of dancing around Travis."

"Sorry," I muttered.

He didn't reply, and I didn't attempt to fill in the silence. The only time we fought was when Travis came up. So why did he keep coming up? I hated this.

"I'm afraid. You know that. I rushed into things with Travis."

"Why can't you let him go?"

I threw my hands up. "I can. I have."

"And yet he still keeps coming up," Luke said.

I scowled. "It doesn't mean anything."

His voice got louder. "Then what is the reason? If you're over him, why can't you commit yourself to me?"

"I can commit myself to you," I said, exasperated. "I have. I consider you my boyfriend."

"You're always holding back. It's like you never totally trust yourself with me."

"I do. I trust you."

"I didn't say trust me, I said trust yourself *with* me. I'm not Travis."

"I never said you were," I whispered, feeling panic rising in my throat. My eyes stung.

"You don't have to say it."

His words felt like a slap in the face. "What does that mean?" I said.

"It's like you're waiting for me to hurt you."

"Can you blame me?" I burst out. How could he not understand? "I *loved* him, and he didn't stay! Can you blame me for being cautious? I never want to go through what I went through after Travis. I have to make sure." My eyes filled with tears, and one escaped. I angrily wiped it away.

"This is so frustrating. Why do you always hesitate?"

I held my hands out helplessly. "I don't want to."

"But you do."

"I'm happy with you, and I don't want to lose you. I need to be sure about how I feel."

"You *know* how you feel. You just won't *admit* how you feel," Luke said forcefully.

I was starting to feel attacked. "So?"

"So maybe you should trust me and let me in."

"Maybe I don't want to. Maybe I'm afraid that if I admit it, I'll just get hurt again. That's *why* I need to make sure."

"How much surer do you need to be?" Luke asked. He stood up and started walking to the door.

"Luke. Wait." I hurried to stop him. "I'm sorry."

"You're sorry? About what?"

I put my hand on the door, hoping he wasn't going to leave. "I didn't mean to make you mad."

"You know, Sophia, I'm a patient guy, and I can wait, but if you can't even be honest with yourself, then what's the point? I'm supposed to hang around being the nice guy while you go on being ambivalent? This is me. Take it, or leave it. I love you. But if you're not going to let yourself feel the same because you don't trust me, why are you even bothering being here?"

He pulled open the door with such force that I stepped back, but I grabbed his arm, which stopped him. He stood there, his body angled away. "I care for you, Luke. You know I do." I had to make him understand.

He looked directly at me. "Yeah, but I *love* you. And there's a big difference."

I had screwed up.

"I'll just leave you alone until you make up your mind," he said, looking straight ahead instead of at me.

"Are you giving me an ultimatum?"

"You figure it out." He let out a bitter laugh, pulled out of my grasp, and shook his head as he walked away.

Chapter Eighteen
You Live with Your Buts, and His But's Not Bad

I RAN AWAY.

I know, really mature of me.

I left without even saying good-bye, though I did leave a note saying I was sorry. Staying in the casita made my escape easy and discreet. I couldn't stop crying and didn't want anyone to know.

Not one of my finer moments.

I debated with myself as I drove away. Was I emotionally invested in the relationship? Yes. Otherwise, I wouldn't be crying like this.

But was I acting like Travis? I didn't think so, but from Luke's point of view, my ambivalence could be perceived as a lack of commitment. But lack of commitment wasn't the problem. Maybe Luke was working hard to move this relationship forward, and I was just stalling.

Did I love him? Well, I was pretty sure I did. Could I tell him? No. Could I see myself marrying him? Okay . . . yes. But marriage? Yikes. Scary big huge commitment. What if it didn't work out again? What if Luke left me like Travis did? Would Luke do that? I wanted to believe he wouldn't.

Were there serious issues with him? No. Red flags? Not really. The only hang-up I could find was my residual Travis baggage. But that was my issue, not his. And that would eventually go away, right? Maybe? The scars would fade. It would just take time. I needed more time.

Was it commitment or trust that I had a problem with? I was committed to Luke, so was it really a trust issue? Did I not trust him? I thought I did. Maybe just not with my heart. Hadn't he proved himself? Or maybe I just didn't trust myself.

It wasn't like I was guilty of convincing myself he was a great guy, but . . . he was a great guy. He wasn't arrogant like Travis. In fact, he was almost the opposite of Travis. He was kind. He was thoughtful. He took care of me. Maybe I'd forgotten too easily what a great guy Luke was. Did I take all that for granted?

Not to mention he was good looking. I couldn't forget that or take that for granted. It was way more than physical though. I liked him. I liked his family. His mom was great. But most of all, he had seen me at the lowest point in my life and still liked me.

But marriage? Yikes, still. The thought of failure continued to scare me. More like terrify me.

I needed backup. Reinforcements. I needed to call in the troops, or trooper, to help me beat a dead horse.

"Gretchen?" I said after she picked up on the other end.

"Hey," she said, surprised. "What's going on?"

"Well . . . I'm driving home."

"Right now? But I thought you were staying until Sunday."

"We sort of had a fight," I answered sheepishly.

Sort of? Who was I kidding? Certainly not myself.

She yawned. "About what?"

Did I wake her up? I looked at the clock: 8:30 a.m. It felt like I had been up for hours. I already wanted to call it a day. "Us. Me. Fitting in with his family. Commitment."

"Wait, wait, wait," she said. "Start over."

"Okay." I took a deep breath. "Basically I've never told Luke I love him."

"Really?" She sounded shocked.

"Yes." Was that so unbelievable?

"Has he told you he loves you?"

"Yes. Just this weekend. But I think he's wanted to for a while."

"And do you? Love him?"

"Well . . ."

"Then what's the problem?" Gretchen sounded like the answer was obvious.

"He wants more. He's ready to move forward."

"Like marriage?"

I gulped. "Yeah, like marriage."

Her voice softened. "Why is that so bad?"

"What if I'm wrong, Gretch? What if I'm wrong *again*?" I started choking up.

"You can't make the same mistake twice, can you?"

"Gretchen, there are people who have been divorced two, three, four times."

"Sophia, seriously. You're not going to get married four times."

My shoulders slumped. "I know, I know. I'm being dramatic. But . . ."

"But what?"

Wasn't it me who told those various girls from my BYU ward who came up to me for marriage advice that it was the *buts* they'd have to live with? The "I love him, *but* . . ." or "He's a great guy, *but* . . ." When I filled in the blank after my *but*, it was *what if I'm wrong*? What if I did marry Luke and he wanted to leave me? What if there was something wrong with *me* that drove men away? The realization hit me hard. I cut across three lanes and pulled over to the side of the highway as tears filled my eyes and spilled down my cheeks.

"Soph? Are you still there?"

"I'm worried that I drive guys away from me. Maybe I drove Travis away."

"Are you listening to yourself? Travis drove himself away, probably happily in his BMW. You said yourself that with the state you were in when Luke met you, you were surprised it didn't scare him away. Luke's a great guy. You're a great girl. He adores you and is really good to you. *Really* good to you. Good enough that I could say I'm a little jealous. Come on. You're making it harder than it needs to be. Forget all the teenage angst and get to the real stuff."

Wow. Gretchen had gained more than just a testimony in New Zealand. She'd picked up some wisdom and good advice along the way.

I took a deep breath. It was true. She was right.

This was my fault, and only I could fix it.

She continued without waiting for me to answer. "He saw you when you were depressed, and he still stuck around. You said he was the only one you let in, so obviously you trust him. He didn't give up on you even though you were not open to relationships at the time. No one else did what he was able to do." She paused momentarily. "And the thing is, from what you told me, it wasn't even a selfish thing. With Travis, it was kind of a mutual using. He thought you were hot; you thought he was hot. But Travis didn't stick around. He left his mission early; he was a quitter. Luke wasn't interested in you just because you're gorgeous."

I thought about the times Luke had seen me not looking my best, which was actually most of the time. He had seen me many times with unbrushed hair, dressed in sweats and T-shirts. There was nothing attractive about me those days.

"But," I argued, "it was kind of his job. He was elders quorum president *and* our home teacher."

"Cut it out. Stop making excuses. How many guys do you know who are that motivated by a sense of duty? There was something about you that held his attention, and it wasn't just your looks."

I was frustrated with myself. Gretchen was right. I knew that. Now if I could just make myself do something about it.

I stayed parked in the breakdown lane for a few more minutes to pull myself together and gather my thoughts. My head was starting to pound, probably because all the tears had dehydrated my brain.

I looked in the rearview mirror to check out the disaster my tears had left and wiped my face as best I could, then I called Luke.

Because I was such a chicken, I kind of sort of hoped it would go to voice mail and I could just leave an apology there. Another really mature moment. But it didn't go as hoped, and Luke picked up after the first ring.

"Luke?" I gulped.

"Where *are* you?" It was a cross between irritated and worried.

"I, uh, went for a drive to clear my head." I stumbled over my excuse. I knew it was poor.

"So you did leave." Again, I couldn't tell if he sounded accusatory or relieved.

Had he been looking for me?

"Are you coming back?" Luke asked carefully.

I didn't answer. I was working up the courage.

"Well?"

The ball was in my court. He was leaving it all up to me. "I think you're right. I need to figure things out."

Way to wimp out, I know.

Chapter Nineteen

Quarantined

BY THE TIME I MADE it home, I was a complete mess. I had cried most of the way, and as a result I had a pounding headache.

My mom was surprised to see me. "How come you're home?"

The floodgates opened again as I started to cry once more. "Luke and I got in a fight, and I left."

"You just left?" Disbelief shone in her eyes.

"Yes." I didn't meet her gaze. Instead, I looked away and wiped the tears off my face.

"And Luke was okay with that?"

"Luke didn't know until I was already gone."

My mom nodded slowly as if processing the information. "What was the fight about?"

"Love. Marriage. Us."

"Why are you fighting about that?"

I threw up my hands. "I don't know, Mom. We just are. I have baggage, and I can't move on."

"The best way to—"

"Mom, I just can't handle being positive about this right now." I knew it was rude before I even said it. "My head hurts, and for some random reason, my stomach has a rash that is itching like crazy. I am probably breaking out in hives because of the stress. I'm tired, and I'm going back to bed. I will deal with everything later when I don't feel so terrible."

My mom looked like she had been slapped. "Well, okay. If that's the way you feel about things, then fine."

And there was one more person I would have to apologize to.

Before I climbed into bed, I texted Luke to let him know I had made it home safely. Not surprisingly, he didn't text back.

I woke up feeling strange. I still had a headache just big enough to be nagging but not pounding enough to need medicine. I gulped down a whole bottle of water, thinking I was dehydrated and the water would make the headache go away. I fell back asleep before I could tell if it had helped or not.

I woke up to my Mom's cool hand on my cheek. "Soph?"

"Uh-huh?" I felt groggy.

"Do you feel okay? You've been sleeping for almost five hours."

"Is that bad?" In my haze, I couldn't figure out why she was waking me up. "I'm cold and achy."

"I think you have a fever."

"Maybe," I mumbled. It was too much work to shake the sleep-induced haze. I rolled over and pulled the covers over me.

I must have dozed off again because I woke to my mom talking to me again. "Sophia?" Mom was asking, her soft hand on my forehead. "How about we give you some medicine?"

"Okay," I agreed, still half asleep. Why was I so tired?

She sat on the edge of my bed and helped prop me up. "Here's some Advil. I'll hold the drink."

I swallowed dutifully and promptly burrowed under the covers again.

"You must have picked something up. Maybe a little heat stroke?" I heard Mom say. I think she turned out the lights as they left, but I wasn't sure.

I don't know how long I slept, but the next time I woke Mom was talking to me. "I think you have the chicken pox," she said.

"What?" I peeled my eyes open to see Mom and Dad standing next to the bed, staring down at me.

"Chicken pox," Mom repeated. "Cali called and said Joy has the chicken pox. It's going around her playgroup."

"Didn't I ever get immunized for chicken pox?"

"Oh, no, I never had you immunized. I thought it was silly, and I wanted you to get them," my mom answered—quite cheerfully, I might add.

"I think I finally got them," I said, flopping back onto my pillow.

* * *

I was in bed for four days with a combination of fever and red spots that were blistering bumps. The first two days were the worst—my fever was

102.4, I had flulike symptoms, and I did nothing but stay in bed. Day three the fever was more low-grade, but the rash was everywhere, and I mean everywhere: eyelids, ears, between my toes, in my hair, and on my lips. They were even in my nose and throat. I kept myself quarantined and used it as an excuse not to pull on my big-girl pants and call Luke. I wasn't ready to deal with that quite yet.

"Hey, Soph," Dan said. "You look like you slept with fleas."

"I feel like it too," I said, rubbing my arm with the palm of my hand. "They're itching like crazy."

"That's what they do."

I looked at him. "Are you sure you want to be that close to me? You might accidentally touch me."

"And?"

"You might catch them too," I said.

"I won't get them. I was immunized."

I stared at Dan. "What?"

"I was immunized."

"Why were you immunized and I wasn't?" It didn't make any sense to me.

"Because I had to before I went on my mission. It's part of the rules." Dan made an *Oh well* gesture with his hands.

"That's so not fair."

"One of the blessings of serving a mission, I guess," Dan said.

I faked a smile. "Must be nice."

My mom stood in the doorway. "Time for more calamine?" She held up the bottle and a bag of cotton balls.

"Yes, please. That would be great, Mom."

My mom helped me as best she could with applying calamine lotion to the spots I couldn't reach. My appearance didn't improve much. Now I was chalky white. But at least my comfort level improved. Coupled with some Benadryl, the calamine soon took effect, and I was feeling a little better.

"That should keep you covered for a while." My mom stood up.

I put my hand on her arm. "Thanks, Mom, for everything. Sorry I snapped at you when I got back from California."

She patted my arm. "You're welcome, honey."

After about five days, I thought I was better until I woke up the next morning completely scabbed over. Trust me, there was nothing at all attractive about the chicken pox. I looked disgusting. That was the only way to describe all the nasty scabs. And some of the rash had yet to scab over. I was so tempted to pick them all off but was able to control myself with my fear of the pock-mark scar.

I didn't need any more scars. I had enough emotional ones as it was.

* * *

After a couple more days, I was finally able to drag myself out of bed. I checked my phone for any calls or texts from Luke, but there weren't any. I thought I would test the waters by sending him a benign text. *Sorry I took off and left things the way I left them.*

He didn't answer right away. In fact, he didn't answer until the next day. *OK.*

He was going to make things difficult. Correction: I had made things difficult, and I needed to fix them. He wasn't going to make things easy. But, at the same time, I didn't deserve easy. I could at least offer my excuse for being out of touch for so long. *I got the chicken pox when I came home. I have been in bed ever since.*

He texted back later that night. *So did Mark's kids. You probably got it from them since they have never been immunized. April seems slightly embarrassed and somewhat appalled that you got it from her kids.*

I immediately texted him. *I feel bad because I'm pretty sure I gave it to them. Joy got it from her playgroup. I think I infected everyone down there. I hope dogs can't catch the chicken pox. Kimmy might never forgive me if I gave Einstein this dreaded disease.*

Do you need me to come up?

I thought about calling him right then and blaming my behavior on being feverish, but I knew that wasn't the truth. I was doing what I did best and was overanalyzing everything and letting my baggage get the best of me. I just wanted more time to figure out what I wanted and then tell Luke. I texted him instead. *Thanks, but no. My mom is taking care of me, and I am a mess.*

Chapter Twenty
Suddenly in a Mess and in Way over My Head

AFTER TEN DAYS OF BEING sick, I ventured out of my room a big scabby mess in search of food. I finally had my appetite back, and I was famished. Dan was in the kitchen, leaning against the counter, talking on the phone. Before I'd even made it to the fridge, I could tell by the look on Dan's face that all was not well with him. He looked sick. I was hoping it had to do with his call and not my chicken-pox appearance.

"I want to, but I can't just take off from work right now. The soonest I could get there would be next weekend, and I know that's not soon enough," he said.

He stood and started pacing back and forth. "Maybe I can take Wednesday off, fly up Tuesday night, and come back Wednesday night."

There was another moment of quiet. I could hear the person's voice on the other end of the line just well enough to know it was Rhonda.

"I know, I know. I'll see what I can do and get there as soon as possible, okay? Love you too. Bye." He hung up and looked at me. "I thought you were getting better."

"I am."

"Well, yeah, but you still look . . ."

"Revolting? Why, thank you, Dan. I love you too." I walked toward him like I was going to hug him.

He instinctively leaned away. "I wasn't going to say revolting. You just look bad, that's all. Have you sent a picture to Luke?"

"I haven't talked to him since I got home. Besides, I really wouldn't want him to see me like this. I don't want to scare him away."

"He would have run a long time ago if he was easily scared," Dan said.

I knew he was joking, but I couldn't laugh. I was the one who was running away.

"What's the matter, sis?"

I busied myself with looking for something to eat in the fridge. "Mom hasn't filled you in?" The cool air felt good against my burning cheeks.

"Are you two following in my footsteps?" His voice took on a teasing tone.

"I think Luke would like to."

When I shut the fridge door and turned, Dan was looking at me, his eyebrows lifted in curiosity. "What about you?"

I chewed on the corner of my lip, owning my new truth. "Yeah, I'm, uh, not quite there yet."

He cocked his head. "Not quite where?"

"I'm not ready to talk marriage. I don't want to rush anything like I did with Travis."

"You know what I notice is different this time around? You don't have to justify Luke's behavior. With Travis, you were always making excuses for him. You don't do that with Luke."

I thought about it. Dan had a point that I hadn't considered before. "You are absolutely right," I said.

"So you *will* be following in my footsteps." Dan's mouth turned up into a satisfied grin.

I went into the family room and sank into the couch. "We'd have to be talking to do that." I let my head loll on the back cushion.

Dan sat down beside me. "Uh-oh. Trouble in paradise?"

"Yeah," I admitted, turning my head to look over at him. "Let's get through your wedding first though. From your phone conversation, it sounds like there might be some bumps in the road," I commented carefully because I couldn't tell if they were fighting or if it was something else.

Dan sank into the couch and ran his hands through his hair. "Rhonda was in a car accident this morning."

"Is she okay?" I asked, worried.

"She broke her ankle, but other than that, she's okay. Her mom was with her and broke two ribs. The car was totaled."

"What happened?"

"Someone ran a red light, and Rhonda was making a left turn. They're lucky they weren't hurt more than they were, but she's pretty shaken."

"She wants you to come up?" I guessed that was the conversation I had walked in on.

"Yes, and I want to go up, but we have a big project going on at work right now, and I can't take any time off. I might be able to get Wednesday off, but if not, it'll have to wait until the weekend."

"That's not soon enough? Rhonda's got to understand."

"She does, but because of the accident, she's freaking out about the wedding and—"

"The wedding? Why? She can still get married with a broken ankle. Her dress will hide the cast, and I'll cover her crutches with glitter if that will make her feel better."

Dan smiled. "I might take you up on that. But she thinks maybe we should put the wedding off because she won't have things pulled together for the reception down here, and with her mom hurt . . . I don't know, Soph. She's being all dramatic and emotional and crying, and I don't know what to tell her. Who cares about the reception? I just want to marry her in two and a half weeks."

"That's so sweet."

"Yeah, well, she didn't seem to think so. When I told her that, she started crying even more."

"She's a girl. She's a girl who is very passionate about her parties. She's a girl who loves all things Disney. She has probably dreamed of a fairy-tale wedding since she was a little girl, and any blip in that plan is a total disaster in her mind. What about Mom? Have you talked to her? She helped me pull my reception together pretty quickly." Like, in six weeks, to be exact.

"You haven't heard, have you?" Dan looked at me.

I blinked, confused. "What? Is there something more about Rhonda?"

"No, about Mom."

"What about Mom?" I asked slowly.

"She got called into the bishop's office last night."

I waited. "And what did he want?"

"Guess who's going to be the new Relief Society president?"

"No!" I gasped.

"Yup."

"You're kidding! That is, wow, that's heavy-duty responsibility . . . and really bad timing."

"I know."

"And with Mom working full-time and now this, she's not going to have much free time to pull together a reception."

"Yeah, exactly, which is part of the reason Rhonda is freaking out, and I don't know how to reassure her. I can't guarantee everything is going to work out fine. I've never planned a reception before. I don't know what I'm doing."

"Yeah, but I have done it before, and that's what you're going to do, or, I should say, that's what I'm going to do."

"What? I'm not following you."

"I'll finish planning your reception here." I mean, how much work could it be? Knowing Rhonda, it was probably almost completely done.

"Seriously?"

"Completely."

"That is the best news I've heard all day. Wait until I tell Rhonda."

He called her back right then. "Hey, honey, good news. Sophia said she would take care of pulling the reception together here."

He was silent for a moment, then looked over at me. "Let me put her on." He handed me the phone.

"Hey, Rhonda. How are you? How's the ankle feeling?"

"Sophia. I can't believe this is happening to me. I'm so worried we will have to postpone the wedding." She was sounding a little hysterical. Maybe she was on pain killers. But it was her wedding she was talking about, so I had to give her a break. After all, if this had happened before I'd married Travis, I would have been freaking out too.

"Dan said the reception here wasn't completely planned."

"Yes. I can do some, but I don't think my mom is up for helping. And without a car, it'll be hard for me to get down there to pull it together."

"I could do it. You wouldn't have to worry about a thing."

It sounded like Rhonda gulped. "Like, everything?" I could tell she wasn't fully on board with my idea.

"That's exactly what I was thinking."

"Do you think you could handle it?"

Okay, she was definitely doubting my idea. "Rhonda, I get the impression my suggestion makes you nervous."

She hesitated. "Just a little."

"Trust me; it'll be great."

There was silence on the other end.

This really wasn't the way I'd imagined the conversation would go. I thought she would be thrilled that I was willing to step in and take care of things. "Do you trust me?"

"Well, honestly, no."

"Really?"

"Well, it's not like you cook, and—"

"Rhonda, I know how to cook. I just didn't cook," I reminded her. "Besides, I don't really think cooking is a requirement for this."

"I don't want it to be a buffet of Pop Tarts and Diet Coke. Or store-bought rolls and a wedding cake from Smith's."

I bit my tongue. I was starting to get offended.

"I don't know. It's a lot of work on short notice, and what if you can't do it?"

She was worried I would plan a disaster. Here I thought I was doing something nice and noble, and she didn't want to take me up on my offer.

I needed a breather or to put myself in time-out or something. I reminded myself I was trying to be helpful, but this was her wedding and her call, and emotions tended to run high when a wedding was on the line. "Why don't you think about it, and you and Dan can make a decision?" I suggested.

I handed the phone back to Dan without waiting for her response. I had a sudden wave of emotions, and my eyes filled with tears. It hurt that I was trying to do a good thing and was being rejected.

My brother stood up and walked into the kitchen. "I think we should," Dan said in a low voice. I wasn't trying to eavesdrop, but I wasn't exactly not listening either.

"Because she's done it before," Dan said. "And it was very nice."

A pause.

"Well, I don't think we have a choice. I don't want to put off the wedding because of a stupid reception. If it's because you're in too much pain, I get that, but not because of a reception."

I heard Dan make an impatient noise. "Why are you blowing this out of proportion? Sophia can handle it, and I think we should let her." There was silence for a moment, then, "Fine!"

It sounded like Dan threw something.

I went into the kitchen to find him sitting with his arms crossed, a scowl on his face, the phone across the room on the floor.

"Sorry, I didn't mean to cause a fight. I thought Rhonda would be happy about it."

"She should be. I know I am."

"Well, let me know what you two decide." I forced my voice to sound upbeat and pasted a smile on my face.

"Okay," Dan said without even looking at me.

I turned to leave.

"Hey, Sophia?" Dan said.

I turned back around.

"Thanks for the offer. I really appreciate it. I'll talk to Rhonda about it later."

"Sure, Dan. No problem."

* * *

Dan knocked on my bedroom door a couple of hours later.

"Hey," I said as I opened the door.

"Rhonda and I came to a decision," he said.

"Oh, yeah? What's that?" I had nearly talked myself out of volunteering to do their reception. It was easier to convince myself I really didn't want to do it in the first place than to admit my feelings were hurt and I was feeling unappreciated.

"We would be grateful if you would take care of the reception."

"Really?" I let out a surprised laugh. "I didn't think Rhonda was going to give in on this one."

Dan's lips became a tight line. "I told her I wouldn't agree to changing the wedding because of the reception, so either you did it, or we just skipped it and went immediately on our honeymoon."

"And she agreed?" It didn't sound like Rhonda.

"Eventually," Dan admitted.

"Ah. So . . ."

"Yeah. She's not thrilled, but the wedding is still on."

I nodded.

"I hated to give her an ultimatum, but I just want to get married. I'm tired of all the planning and the waiting. All I care about is having it done."

"Yeah, there is a lot of pomp and fanfare leading up to the wedding. Most of it doesn't matter, but that perspective takes time to realize. So just keep reminding her how excited you are to marry her and try to humor the rest of the details. It will all work out."

"Life goes on, I guess." He sighed.

"With or without the perfect wedding."

"If only Rhonda felt that way."

The wheels started turning in my mind as soon as he left the room. If I was going to do this, what would I need? I'd have to talk to one of them to see what had already been taken care of and then figure out the rest. I'd have to find out what their budget was and how to pay for everything. Most importantly, I would have to wing it and make it look like it hadn't been planned on a whim, but I was pretty sure I could do it.

Besides, this was the biggest party of Rhonda's life. Surely she'd already planned it down to the minute and I would just have to step in to coordinate and execute, right?

My cell phone rang, and Gretchen's name came up on the screen. "Can I hitch a ride with you to Provo when you go? I want to bring some stuff up early. Do you think your other roommate will mind if I store things there for a couple of weeks?

I was too distracted to think about what I was saying. "Um, I think that will be good."

"You sound weird."

"Well, suddenly I have a wedding reception to plan."

"Luke proposed?" Gretchen screamed.

I thought about what I had said and what it must have sounded like. "Oh, no, sorry. It's Dan and Rhonda's thing here. Rhonda got into a car accident, and—"

"Is she okay?"

"Yeah, but she broke her ankle, and her mom broke a couple ribs, and Rhonda was freaking out about what to do for the reception down here, so I said I would take care of it."

"That was generous of you. That's huge for you."

Gretchen's reaction was sort of what I had expected from Rhonda. "That might change your return plans to California. I might need your help for the reception," I said.

"I'll help you with it," Gretchen said without hesitation.

"Good, I was hoping I'd be able to recruit you." I smiled.

"Sure. What do you need?"

"I don't think it will be all that big a deal, but plan a couple of days in Vegas."

"Okay, sounds good to me," Gretchen said.

* * *

"Sophia, we have a problem," Dan said on Tuesday evening.

It was never a good thing when someone said there was a problem. "What is it?"

"It's about the reception. There's a big problem."

My heart started pounding. "Like how big?"

"Like we lost our reservation at The Red Carpet Reception Room."

"That's it?" I let out a huge breath.

Dan looked at me strangely. "That's a pretty big deal."

"I thought you were going to tell me the wedding was off."

"No, the wedding is still on; we just have no place to hold the reception. Rhonda was supposed to confirm yesterday, but she forgot because she's taking pain pills and isn't on top of things. So she called the guy today and explained the whole situation and the accident and the painkillers, and the guy told her she had lost her reservation."

"Are you serious? He wasn't willing to work with her at all?"

"Nope." Dan shook his head slowly. "And we lost our deposit."

"I can't believe it. I can't believe that guy was so heartless."

"Now Rhonda's really freaking out. I'm almost afraid to call her. Last time we talked, I made the mistake of telling her to calm down. *Never* tell a hysterical girl to calm down."

I tried to hide my smile. It was so true. "Better to learn that now, before you're married. Trust me, knowing that will come in handy."

"It's like every little thing that goes wrong Rhonda makes it into a huge deal. I mean, what else could go wrong?"

"Don't say that, Dan. You don't want to curse yourself."

"Rhonda feels like nothing is working out, and she can't understand why. I can't deal with any more of her hysterics, but I don't know what to do with the reception."

"I said I would—"

"I know, but with everything bad that's happening, Rhonda is thinking it's some sort of sign that we shouldn't get married."

Wow. Rhonda really was freaking out. And Dan too. I had never seen him this way before. "Dan, there is drama before every wedding. Relax, take a deep breath, and we'll figure things out."

I put my arm on his shoulder and literally forced him to sit on the couch. Then I sat next to him and wondered how we were going to fix this.

"Okay," I said calmly, "first of all, is the ceremony time all scheduled?" I grabbed a pencil and a piece of paper to keep track of the information.

"Yes, 2:00 p.m., August 7."

"Okay. Is there going to be a luncheon or any sort of meal after?"

"Mom suggested we have sandwiches at the house to cut down on costs."

I put a check next to lunch on my list. "We need to find someplace to have the reception."

"Yes."

"How about the church?"

Dan sighed. "If we can still get it."

"Let's try. I'll call the building scheduler."

"Okay."

"How about the food?"

"Came with the reception package."

"That's a problem," I said. "How about the centerpieces? Decorations? Flowers?"

Dan grimaced. "I'm pretty sure the flowers were part of the reception package. I think Rhonda was doing the centerpieces and some extra decorations herself."

The problem was getting bigger.

"And the music? Let me guess, that came with the reception package?"

"Yup."

"How about the wedding cake?"

"I don't know. Rhonda talked about making a huge cheesecake."

Oh dear. Cheesecake?

Okay. I was suddenly in way over my head.

Chapter Twenty-One
Needed: Complete Wedding Reception, STAT

I TURNED TO MY MOTHER for help.

I was desperate.

She was used to doing ten things at once, and because of her PMA, she never got discouraged. Of course, I didn't expect her to take over for me since I was the one who had volunteered, but I hoped she would help. I didn't know if being newly put in charge of every woman in the ward was one of those rare instances when my mother would get overwhelmed.

"When will you be sustained?" I asked.

"In two weeks."

"Right before the wedding." I vocalized what I'm sure she was thinking. She had a lot of decisions to make regarding her church responsibilities and didn't have much free time to spend getting ready for the wedding.

"I have to give them names for my counselors by next Sunday. Then the whole presidency will be called in two weeks. If I wasn't teaching summer school—"

"You would be climbing the walls going crazy because you wouldn't be busy." I knew my mother.

"I just didn't expect this calling," my mom said. She let out a sigh. "I haven't finished my classroom for when school starts."

"And has Dan filled you in on the wedding drama?"

"Most of it. You're now in charge of the reception here."

"Sounds like it."

She patted my knee. "If anyone can step in and pull it off, it's you."

I knew I was on my own when she didn't offer her help. I went into my room and momentarily panicked. What was I thinking volunteering to do this? I thought I had finally officially lost my mind.

I just needed a moment, or a day, and then I'd get over it.

I fully enjoyed that moment, then I pulled myself together, sat down, and made a "to do" list. I reviewed what Dan and I had discussed: location, food, flowers, decorations, music, and centerpieces. So basically everything. I flopped back on my bed and stared at the ceiling while giving myself a little pep talk. I could do this. I just needed to tackle one thing at a time.

First on the list was location. I called the building coordinator for our church house and left a message on her answering machine. Luck was on my side because she called me right back. Unfortunately our building was already scheduled for something else. Dang!

But she gave me the number of the building coordinator of the stake center. I was able to get a hold of that person, and she said the building was free that night, so I reserved it. One down, everything else to go.

Food. I didn't know what to do for food. Mine had been catered, and I wasn't about to do all the food myself. I could ask Kimmy to do it, but that would be weird asking her to come to another state to cater a wedding for her brother-in-law's girlfriend's brother's wedding. And since Luke and I weren't talking, I couldn't ask Luke to ask her. Maybe I would see if that was something my mom could manage to be in charge of. I skipped that on the list and went to the next thing: flowers, decorations, and centerpieces. Hmm. I would have to check with Rhonda about flowers. I assumed she had her bouquet taken care of, so I needed to know if she wanted actual flowers at the reception. And I needed to find out her plans for the wedding cake. I decided to put that off until tomorrow. From what Dan had said, Rhonda was hysterical, and I couldn't handle dealing with her right now.

I went onto Pinterest and checked out tons of wedding ideas. Three hours, a bunch of e-mails to Rhonda, and a case of eye strain later, I knew what I was going to do. I felt confident it would be okay. For me and for her.

The next thing I did was call Bradley Benson. I needed a favor, or more like a parachute.

Since my mother was going to be the new Relief Society president, I didn't have to check on tablecloths; I could just ask her.

We had twenty fake trees, strings and strings of twinkle lights, and a box of hurricane vases from my wedding reception that were just sitting in storage. Out of necessity, they would be used for decorations.

I took care of the music next. We had the closest thing I knew of to a musical prodigy in our ward. At sixteen, he was playing the organ for sacrament meeting and arranging music for the ward choir, as well as directing it. I was hoping I could hit him up for some piano music and then resort to an iPod and a small sound system for dancing. It didn't take any convincing at all to get him to agree to play for the evening at a minimal cost to the reception budget.

I went back downstairs and found my mom. With pleadings just short of begging, I got her to agree to help with the food that night. In turn, I agreed to be her classroom slave for two weeks after the wedding so she would be ready for the new school year.

Last but not least, I left myself a reminder note to have Dan send out an e-mail to notify everyone of the location change.

The next day I was working. I picked up Joy, and we headed out to the craft store. By the time Cali returned home from work that evening, I had everything I needed for the reception. We had gone to several craft stores and picked up Chinese lanterns; silver spray paint; spray-on glitter; and silver, dark gray, and pink ribbons. We had also ordered confetti online.

"So what is this big project you're working on?" Cali asked.

"Dan and Rhonda's wedding reception. Rhonda had a car accident, totaled her car, and broke her ankle, and their plans for the reception here all fell through. I volunteered to pull it together."

Cali's eyebrow went up.

"I know. I'm completely crazy for volunteering, but I couldn't not do anything. I mean, he's my brother; she's my roommate."

"I'm impressed."

I smirked. "Don't be yet. You can tell me how impressed you are once it actually happens."

"Still, that's a pretty big favor."

"It's not even a favor. They didn't ask; I offered."

"I'm trying to compliment you, and you're not making it very easy."

"Oh, sorry," I said. I wasn't fishing for compliments.

"So, tell me about it."

I launched into my plans, glad to be able to discuss it with her. I was curious what her opinion of my plans would be, especially since I was secretly pretty excited about them. "Although I'm not sure what to do about the food yet. I don't want to be in charge of it on site because it would tie me down with the responsibility of it for the whole evening. I asked my mom to be in charge of that and maybe ask the Relief Society for help."

"How about I get the young women to help with it?"

"Like make it?"

"No, help set it up, make sure it's replenished. Make sure there are plenty of forks, napkins, and plates. Stuff like that. We'll call it a service project that will count toward their Personal Progress certificate."

"That would be awesome. Then my mom wouldn't have to deal with that part."

"If you figure it out as quickly as you pulled the decorations together, you'll have it done in no time."

"I hope so." I really, *really* hoped so.

Chapter Twenty-Two
Hit Upside the Head

THE DAYS LEADING UP TO Dan and Rhonda's wedding were fast-paced and frenzied. Gretchen and I drove up to Provo Tuesday night. Rhonda was going to the Salt Lake Temple on Wednesday and her bridal shower was that night at her mom's house. Thursday we would drive back down to Vegas with Ashlee to go to the wedding.

I saw an unexpected familiar face as I was walking up to my old apartment. "Justin! What are you doing here? I thought you were in Alaska doing the fishery thing." I gave him a hug as he came over to me.

Justin made a "hmp" sound. "That lasted like three weeks. The smell was so bad I don't think I can ever look at raw fish again. It was really long, weird hours, and it never gets dark there, so it was hard to sleep. I couldn't even date the girls. They smelled like fish. Even their hair smelled like it."

"It was that bad?"

He nodded emphatically. "I threw my clothes away because I couldn't get the fish smell out."

"But you made good money, right?"

"I spent more on airline tickets than I made at my job."

I chuckled. "You should cross fisherman off your list of potential careers."

He laughed.

"Even the shortage of men there couldn't keep you?"

"Turns out I had my facts backwards. The men outnumber the women, not the other way around."

"Do you think you're going to try the Hawaiian pineapple plantations next? They're supposed to pay big money too."

Justin grinned. "I'm going to stick with my minimum-wage job here at BYU until school starts. At least the girls in Provo don't smell." He looked back at the parking lot. "Did Luke drive up with you?"

"No, he's in California right now."

"Didn't you go see him when he got back from Europe?"

"I did. I met all his family too."

"Hope you get along well with them. You might become one of them." He gave me a little jab with his elbow. "Huh? Am I right? Things seem to be picking up speed."

I was not going to fall for Justin's casual attempt to pry. He was a good guy, but I had a hard enough time discussing the relationship with Luke; I certainly wasn't going to get into it with Justin. Especially now. "Oh, you know." I shrugged nonchalantly. "Things are"—I searched for an apt word—"good." Okay, I knew they weren't good.

"*Good* good or just good?"

"Justin." I took a deep breath. I didn't want to tell him about the fight.

"How good is good?" He raised his eyebrows, still prying.

I found a way to shift the conversation slightly. "You know you sound just like a girl. You need to find yourself a girlfriend so you won't be so consumed with our relationship."

"It doesn't hurt to ask." He pretended to be wounded.

I tried a different angle. "You know when it's your turn, I am going to tease you just as mercilessly."

"I'm only doing it because I love you. Can you blame me for wondering? You guys are always so secretive."

"It's easier that way when you have a lurid past like mine."

"I don't even know what that word means."

"Shocking. Dramatic."

"Yes, you seem to have quite a dramatic life," Justin said. "Hey, I hear Rhonda is joining your family."

"Yep. She and my brother hit it off, and now they're getting married really soon."

"And how do you feel about Rhonda being your sister-in-law?"

"I'm not sure, but it's not like she's going to be my wife. My brother will probably put on a ton of weight."

Justin nodded. "I'll miss all the treats she and Ashlee used to bring us."

I placed my hand on his shoulder and tried to keep my face straight. "I'm sure Ashlee will still bring you treats—all the cheesecake you can eat."

"She's so young and . . . chatty." Justin grimaced.

"She is, but I learned a couple of things that made me understand her a little better."

"Oh yeah? Like what?"

"She's the only member in her family, and her parents don't support her membership in the Church. She moved to Provo to be around others who share her same belief."

"Hmm." Justin nodded. "But that doesn't explain her over-the-top enthusiasm."

"That's just part of who she is."

"Still. She's not my type." He emphatically shook his head. "Is Luke going to Rhonda's wedding? Ashlee is trying to rope me into going, but I haven't committed yet. I guess it wouldn't be so bad if Luke was there and I could hang out with you guys. I would have to catch a ride with you if I go."

"Yes, of course you can catch a ride. But I'm not sure if Luke is going," I said.

Justin stopped and gave me an intense look. "What's the deal, Sophia? Did you break up?"

"No. Not exactly."

"What does that mean?"

I cringed. "I don't know. Exactly."

"Really, what's up? You two were like love at first sight in the laundry room."

"Yeah, I know. I just . . ." I didn't want to explain to Justin that it was because I was afraid. Afraid of myself.

"The way Luke was talking at the end of the semester, I thought for sure you'd be marr—" Justin looked at me. My expression must have stopped him. I'm sure my eyes were huge. "You know what? Never mind."

"Ah, we'll sort it out once I come to my senses." I sounded like I was joking, but I wasn't.

* * *

Justin unexpectedly called me the next morning just as I got out of the shower.

"Could you give me a ride?" he asked.

"Sure. Where?"

"Actually, I need you to pick me up and give me a ride home. I'm at the east entrance of the Wilk." Then he hung up. I didn't even get to tell him it would take a couple of minutes before I could go. I still needed to get dressed and dry my hair.

I was barely finished getting ready when I heard the front door open. It was Gretchen. She set her bags from the bookstore on the table with a confused look on her face. "The weirdest thing just happened on campus."

"Oh, yeah? What?" I asked while checking my hair in the mirror.

"I was crossing Campus Drive, you know, coming out of the bookstore, walking toward the parking lot, and this guy was riding his bike and texting or something and totally rode right into the back of a bus."

"He hit the bus?" I was momentarily distracted from applying my lip gloss.

"Yeah, but the crazy thing is he looked at me—like we made eye contact—then he took his phone out and crashed into the bus."

"Did you know him?"

"I don't think so. But he looked directly at me. It was weird to make eye contact and then have him immediately involved in an accident."

"What happened then?" It *was* a little bizarre. It wasn't every day someone witnessed another person crash into a bus.

"I rushed over to make sure he was okay. Cars stopped, people came from where they were waiting at the bus stop, the bus driver got off, the bus emptied. People literally swarmed around him. Then the ambulance came."

"I missed quite a scene. Did he go to the hospital?"

"No, I don't think so. I hung around until the ambulance got there. They seemed to think he was coherent enough, but he kept rambling on about something. I don't think he hit his head on the bus or ground, but he did fall off when the bike hit the bus. Really bizarre. But cute guy."

"How embarrassing. See? It's a good thing I don't know how to ride a bike because that would be me. I would be the person who rode into a bus. I can't imagine riding into a bus when there's no one around to see me, never mind a bunch of people."

"Yeah," Gretchen agreed but seemed distracted.

"Wanna go up to campus with me? I have to pick up Justin. He just called and said he needed a ride." I shrugged. "Although I'm not sure why."

"Who's Justin?"

"Luke's best friend."

"I think I'll stay here."

"Okay. I'll be back soon."

I drove across Ninth East and pulled into the BYU parking lot right across from the Wilk. It was strange to me that Justin wanted me to pick him up when we lived practically across the street from campus. Maybe he had done his book shopping for fall semester early and couldn't carry everything home.

The closer I walked toward the Wilk and saw the accident Gretchen had told me about come into view, the more I wondered if Justin had been involved in it. But I had never seen Justin ride a bike. I didn't even know if he owned a bike.

Sure enough, it was Justin. There he was, in the middle of the whole crowded scene, sitting on the back end of an ambulance, the doors wide open. He was holding an ice pack to his forehead with one hand and was holding some papers in another. He looked okay, meaning he wasn't bloodied and seemed to be carrying on a conversation with the EMT.

"Hey, what happened?" I asked as I walked over to him.

"I saw the most beautiful girl."

I shook my head. "No, I'm talking about the accident."

"Yeah, me too."

"Justin, is your head okay?" I asked.

"Yeah. I was wearing a helmet."

I wasn't understanding. "But what does the girl have to do with the accident?"

I remembered what Gretchen told me about making eye contact with the guy right before he crashed into the bus. "Oh, I get it. You were looking at the girl, got distracted, and hit the bus."

"Actually, I was trying to take a picture of her on my phone, then I hit the bus," Justin admitted.

"I hope you got the picture," I said.

"Yeah, I did." Justin held up his phone.

I couldn't pass up a chance to razz Justin. "That's Gretchen."

"You *know* her?"

"Lucky for you, she's going to be my roommate this fall."

"How come I haven't seen her before?" He blinked a couple times, like he was trying to remember.

"She just got back from her mission."

"Can you introduce me to her?"

"I think you already did that when you hit the bus in front of her today. But, yes, I can formally introduce you. She's at my apartment right now. We'll probably be over later today. Somebody needs to check on you and make sure you don't have a concussion."

"You should definitely do that," Justin said.

I looked around at the scene. "Do you need to hang out here any longer, or are you good to go?"

"I can go. I filled out my accident report for the police and have my instructions from the EMT." He held up the papers.

I glanced over at Justin's crumpled bike on the sidewalk. "What about that?" I pointed to it. "Do we need to take that home?"

Justin shook his head. "I was just going to leave it and hope someone would take care of it."

"You can't just leave a mangled bike on the sidewalk, Justin," I said.

"Okay," Justin walked over to his bike, picked it up, then set it on top of the closest trash can. "Problem solved," he said as he headed toward the car.

"Where's your helmet?" I looked around.

Justin was already walking. "Who cares? I really want to get out of here."

As we approached my apartment, I asked Justin, "So, do you want to come in and meet Gretchen?"

"Yeah," Justin readily said.

Gretchen was eating a sandwich at the kitchen table when we walked in.

"Hey, you *are* that girl," Justin said as soon as he saw her. He must have had residual confusion from his accident because that was not a typical smooth, charming line he would use.

Gretchen got a confused look on her face, and she glanced at me quickly before looking back at Justin. "What?" she replied slowly.

"I saw you this morning before I hit the bus." His charming grin spread across his face. "I'm Justin, by the way." He put out his hand.

"Gretchen," she said, reaching out to return the handshake. "You poor thing. That was you? What happened?"

"I got distracted. By you."

Nothing like blatant honesty that also doubled as flirting.

Gretchen blushed, then reached up to his forehead and moved his hair just enough to see his injury more closely. "I'm glad you weren't hurt worse and didn't need stitches."

"Yeah." Justin let her touch linger. "That's the first time I've ever ridden into a bus. I'm glad I didn't have to go to the hospital."

Justin's groove was off big time.

"Gretchen's going to be driving to the wedding with me," I informed Justin, knowing he would love it.

"You are?" Justin's enthusiasm was apparent. "Me too."

I guessed he was suddenly decided.

"Yeah, *and* I'm going to be living here in the fall," Gretchen said.

It was like they kept fueling the fire of curiosity for each other. As much as I wanted to hang around and watch Gretchen and Justin's get-to-know-you session, Ashlee and I needed to be in Salt Lake.

* * *

Even being Rhonda's roommate, I had never met her parents, so getting together with them Wednesday night was an experience. I say *experience* because that was exactly what it was. It was something I had to be there for to believe.

My parents drove up from Las Vegas and met me in Salt Lake. I had never gone up to Salt Lake with Rhonda to her house. Maybe that was a good thing. I didn't know if I could have handled so much enthusiasm in my former depressed state.

Rhonda's mother, Jean, shook hands with my mother, and I swear fusion occurred. The melding of two like minds into instant friendship. To be honest, it scared me. As a roommate, Rhonda reminded me a lot of my mother, and Jean was an amped-up version of Rhonda. The fact that these two women were going to be related through their kids' marriage seemed to excite both of them to almost the point of giddiness. Wow. It was a world of difference compared to when Maxine and Boyd met my parents. I would never admit to this out loud, but it was a lot more comfortable meeting Dan's in-laws than it was meeting my ex in-laws.

"Now you just got recently engaged yourself, didn't you?" Jean asked, pumping my hand.

"No, not me." I shook my head, keeping my voice even, thankful Luke was not there.

Jean looked flustered. "Oh dear, I'm sorry. I must have you confused with a different roommate. You're not the one that got married, are you?" Her eyes glanced at my ring finger.

"No, that would be Claire. She married my ex-husband." I almost got a little sick pleasure out of telling people that. Because it was too bizarre to be true. And seeing people's reactions was always amusing.

Jean wrinkled her brow. "Well, I am clearly confused."

"Yeah." I laughed, rolled my eyes, and shook my head in disbelief. "Me too."

Clearly confused. That about summed it up. That was how my life had been as of late.

"I'm sorry," Rhonda apologized later as she took me aside. "I didn't tell my mother you were engaged. I said I could see you two getting married. There's a difference, and my mother seems to have missed that."

I had to agree. There was definitely a difference.

Chapter Twenty-Three
Return Road Trip to Vegas

"YOU DIDN'T TELL ME ABOUT Justin," Gretchen said to me giddily the next morning as we were packing up the car.

Probably because I didn't think about Justin. Not in *that* way, at least. I had never thought about playing matchmaker for him. He seemed to do just fine on his own when it came to dating. Plus, considering my track record with Ned and Sarah and their relationship going awry, I wasn't anxious to try again. Gretchen didn't strike me as ditzy or blonde enough to be Justin's type. "Yeah, he's a good guy. Funny, but he's a charmer. Be careful."

She giggled. "He's hot."

If you went for the be-dimpled jock type, then, yes, he was.

"Does he have a girlfriend?"

"Nope. But he's been looking." And maybe he had just found what he was looking for.

Ashlee came bounding down the stairs. She had come back from Salt Lake with me the night before and was up bright and early this morning getting ready for the drive to Vegas. Justin seemed a little dismayed about the six-hour drive with Ashlee.

"Are we actually taking her on another road trip?" Justin asked under his breath. "Have you forgotten the last one? The gum? The games? The excessive talking?"

I silently held up a box of Dramamine. "Got it covered."

Justin let out a visible sigh of relief, and Gretchen looked back and forth between us, trying to figure out what we were talking about.

"Isn't it funny how Dramamine contains the word *drama*, and that's exactly what it's taking care of?" I asked.

"Let's hope it works," Justin replied.

Instead of getting in the front seat, Gretchen offered it to Ashlee. Without waiting for a reply, Gretchen jumped in the backseat. Ashlee looked a bit confused as she slowly climbed in the front seat beside me.

Ashlee was her usual chatty self, but she somehow missed the chemistry brewing between Justin and Gretchen. They were practically emitting pheromones. She started right away with the twenty questions. "Tell us about yourself, Gretchen."

Gretchen shot me a look, suddenly understanding what Justin had been talking about. "Uh, what do you want to know?"

"How do you know Sophia?" I didn't think Ashlee knew what she was doing. She wasn't the only one interested in finding out a little more about Gretchen.

"We were roommates before her marriage and my mission."

Justin saw his in. "You served a mission? Where?"

"New Zealand. How about you?"

"London. With Luke. He was my trainer."

"So that's how you guys know each other."

Justin shifted slightly so he was facing Gretchen more. "We both live in Southern California too. An hour away from each other."

Surprise registered on Gretchen's face. "Me too. Temecula."

Ashlee must have realized she had unintentionally excluded herself from the conversation and undermined her own effort to entice Justin to develop any sort of affection for her. "I'm thinking about serving a mission," Ashlee announced. Her late timing made her announcement sound almost random.

Gretchen glanced at her. "You should. It's a great experience." She then turned her attention back to Justin. "So where exactly in California are you from?"

"Irvine."

"And Luke's from?"

"Vista."

She nodded knowingly. All I knew was if I drove one way, I could get to both Luke's and Gretchen's house in the same trip.

"What are you studying?" Ashlee was desperately trying to get herself back into the conversation.

"I'm an English major," Gretchen answered. "You go to BYU too?" she added, almost as an afterthought.

"No. I go to the Hair Academy."

"Oh, okay," Gretchen said, then turned back to Justin. "Are you a surfer, Justin?"

"Yeah. You?" He turned to her.

She bobbed her head slightly. "Recreational. I'm not that great."

I knew what was coming next.

"We should go. I'll help you," Justin said. And off they went, into the private world of love at first sight, imprinting, can't get enough of each other, speaking in hushed voices.

Ashlee hadn't tried to jump back in. I wondered if she had caught the drift that she wasn't invited to be a part of their exclusive conversation. Apparently so because when I glanced over at her, she had fallen asleep. Dramamine had done its job.

By the time we stopped in St. George to get gas and find someplace to eat, Gretchen was positively giddy. "I really like him."

"I'm glad."

"And what's up with the chatty chick?"

"Ashlee?" I asked.

"Yeah, what's the deal with her?"

"Long story. Rhonda's BFF, always at our apartment, liked Luke, moved on to Justin, the list goes on."

"Did she and Justin date?"

"No. Well, yes. Ashlee has asked Justin out a few times, but Justin isn't interested in her. She's like Rhonda in that respect: she likes testosterone."

Gretchen nodded her head, understanding. Then she looked back at Justin, a dreamy look on her face.

So that was what imprinting looked like.

After we filled the car with gas, at Ashlee's insistence, we went to this weird little restaurant called The Saltine Bucket. I wondered if she had it confused for Cracker Barrel. She insisted she had eaten at one before. I had never heard of it, but it was nothing more than a mom-and-pop diner.

Unfortunately for Ashlee, they only had booths. Gretchen and Justin sat on one side, leaving Ashlee to sit next to me. There was no way Ashlee could win with the Justin situation. Everything she did seemed to benefit Gretchen and Justin, not her.

As I sat, I stepped on something squishy. "Great," I muttered, expecting to find gum stuck to the bottom of shoe. It wasn't gum but a packet of ketchup someone before us had dropped on the floor. It had burst under pressure and shot ketchup all over my other foot.

"Oh, yuck." I swung my leg out to see how bad it was. "I stepped on a ketchup packet."

"Bummer," Justin said as I wiped the mess up with napkins.

When it came time to order, Ashlee was the last one and, for some reason, seemed to ask about everything on the menu.

"Now when you say 'jumbo shrimp,' are they actually shrimp, or are they prawns? And are they boiled or fried? It says the lima beans are prepared with butter and salt. Does that mean they're boiled or steamed? Is there a chance I could switch those out for, say, some edamame? You know, soybeans?"

The waitress snapped her gum but patiently answered all of Ashlee's questions. She wasn't the one getting irritated at Ashlee. We were the hungry ones, and Ashlee was holding up the waitress, which meant she was holding up our order.

"Ashlee, c'mon. Pick something already," Justin encouraged, exasperated.

She scowled at him.

He held up his hands. "I'm starving here."

"Fine. I'll order fish and chips."

Which I thought was weird, since she hadn't even asked about that menu item.

When the food arrived, Justin offered Gretchen a bite of his, giving them a reason to sit closer to each other.

I couldn't tell if Ashlee felt like the situation was uncomfortable, but it didn't seem like it because she started up the conversation again. "How is Rhonda's reception coming along?"

"It's pretty much done. And since you guys are automatically enlisted to help set it up, I'm confident it'll be great."

"That was so nice of you to take over Rhonda's reception." Ashlee turned to Justin. "Don't you think so?"

Justin looked confused. He probably didn't know I was in charge of it until now and probably didn't care. All he knew was I had asked everyone to help with the setup. "Why did you take over the reception?"

"Rhonda and her mom had a car accident," I told him.

"Is she okay?"

I nodded. "She broke her ankle. We're thankful it wasn't worse. I told her I would take care of getting the reception together here."

"Practicing for your own?" Justin asked, his eyebrow raised.

"Nothing planned yet."

"So you just volunteered to take over?" Justin asked.

I shrugged. "It's not that big a deal."

"Rhonda thinks it is," Ashlee said.

"Is that going to be her wedding gift?" Gretchen asked.

"I wasn't really looking at it as a wedding gift," I said.

"But it is very generous," Gretchen said.

I held up my hands. "It's not like I bought them a car or a house or . . . I've planned a reception before; I figured that would be the best thing I could offer them."

"Well, it was really nice," Gretchen said.

Ashlee looked at Gretchen. "Did you know Sophia gave our other roommate, Sarah, her Vera Wang wedding dress?"

"You gave away your Vera Wang?" Gretchen almost looked sad. She had been with me when I'd found it. "That was such a beautiful dress."

"What did your ring look like?" Ashlee asked, getting caught up in the moment.

Gretchen noticed my hesitation because she jumped in. "You don't still have it, do you?"

Now would be a good time to choke or step on another ketchup packet or something.

Justin broke the silence. "Sophia, my fries need some ketchup. Could you pass it, and step on it?" Then he started laughing at his own joke.

"Ha, ha, Justin, very funny." I pretended to not see the humor, but I was really more than grateful for it.

"I think it is," Justin said.

"You have to admit, Sophia, it is just a little bit funny," Gretchen added, smiling at Justin.

So just to be funny back, I picked up one of my fries and chucked it across the table at Justin. Only he ducked, and my fry completely missed him and hit the person sitting on the other side of the booth.

He didn't find it humorous, and neither did his wife.

"I am so sorry," I sputtered when the man and his wife turned around with less-than-amused looks on their faces. "I wasn't trying to hit you; I was trying to . . ."

"Do you not *know* how rude and inappropriate it is to throw food at a restaurant?" the husband demanded.

I could feel my cheeks warming. Of course I knew. All I could do was grovel. "I am so, so sorry."

My apologies weren't sufficient, and it didn't help that Justin and Gretchen kept laughing. The couple, not laughing, reported me to the manager, who sided with the couple, finding my (and I quote) "antics inappropriate" and saying we needed to "vacate the premises immediately."

As soon as the manager left, Justin promptly burst out laughing. Which further infuriated the couple.

"Do you think I could get some to-go containers?" Ashlee asked our disgruntled waitress, who brought the check. Ashlee seemed oblivious to how much the owners wanted us out of their restaurant.

Justin found that hilarious too.

"Shut up, Justin," I hissed. "You're making it worse."

"I can't help it. You got us kicked out of a restaurant called The Saltine Bucket. It sounds so funny. We got kicked out of the bucket. Get it?"

I just wanted to get our walk of shame out of the restaurant over with.

After six hours of driving, we made it to my parents' house. In that time, it had become pretty apparent that Justin and Gretchen were well on their way to a relationship, so I decided to razz him about it. "So, you and Gretchen, huh?" I whispered as we got out of the truck and started grabbing our bags.

He gave an embarrassed smile but said nothing.

"What about Ashlee? Love triangle? Love it."

Justin turned three shades of red, which gave me more than enough satisfaction.

Chapter Twenty-Four
At Least Travis Was Good for Something

THE CONVERSATION WE'D HAD BACK at The Saltine Bucket had given me a great idea. I had something that could potentially be a really nice gift for Dan and Rhonda. Once we arrived at my parents' house, I was anxious to follow through.

I went up to my room and had to search for a few minutes before I finally saw what I was looking for—my ring. The ring I had no reason to keep. I had to crawl under my desk, reach behind my dresser, and inhale a lot of dust to get it. I'm guessing it fell out of my bag at some point. It was time to get rid of it, no matter how much effort it took. I felt good about my decision. It was symbolic of my letting go and moving forward with my current relationship. I was sure Luke wouldn't mind the ring being gone either.

My plan was to turn it in and hopefully get store credit, but I wasn't sure if it was actually possible until I went to the store. Now I just needed to find out from my brother where to go.

Dan wasn't hard to find; I just had to follow the sound of girls' laughter coming from the kitchen. Justin and Gretchen were nowhere to be found, but that was okay; the fewer people around the better. I couldn't come right out and ask him in front of everyone because that would ruin the surprise.

I discreetly pulled him aside. "Hey, where'd you buy Rhonda's ring?" I asked.

"Are you in the market?" His smile was huge.

"Only in the market to sell one off."

He cocked his head. "Huh?"

I excused Dan's confusion on the fact that he was getting married the next day and there was complete mayhem all around us.

"You know, the ring Travis gave me."

"Oh yeah, right, right." He still looked at me suspiciously. "Are you sure you're not shopping for you?"

"Yeah, pretty sure." Luke and I would have to be at least talking before we moved on to ring shopping.

* * *

"Can I sell this ring?" I held it out to the salesman behind the counter at the jewelry store.

"Yes," the guy nodded. "We can buy the ring for current market value, or we can give you store credit for the full value toward another purchase. Usually store credit is more."

"So I can trade this ring in for store credit?" I reiterated, wanting to be sure I was understanding correctly.

"I would have to appraise it, but, yes, we do that."

I handed the ring over to him. He took it and pulled out a magnifying glass. He looked the ring over inside and out, then he weighed it.

"It's one carat," I told him, though, once I thought about it, he probably already knew how big it was.

He punched some numbers in on the calculator. "I can offer you $579 for the gold."

That was not the amount I was expecting. "What about the diamond? What's that worth?"

He looked at me. "Not much since it's a CZ."

"A CZ?" I repeated, not understanding.

"Cubic zirconia. A manmade gem that resembles a diamond."

"It's not real?" My head slowly fell as I processed the information. "It's a fake."

The salesman looked sympathetic. "Yes. Sorry. You didn't know?"

"No. But I'm not shocked." I thought for a second. "You said I'd get more value if I got store credit and used it toward a future purchase?"

"I did. Perhaps you'd like to look around and see if there is anything of interest to you?" he suggested.

Even though selling this ring was equivalent to free money, I didn't want anything that was connected to Travis in any way. I would always think of the bracelet or the earrings as the jewelry I'd bought with Travis's money.

The sales guy stood there, waiting.

"Can I credit it toward someone else?" I held my breath, hoping.

"Who?"

"My brother bought a ring here just over a month ago, and I'm wondering if I can put this credit toward his account."

"That can be arranged. That's a thoughtful gesture," the sales guy said.

The transaction took barely five minutes. Rhonda's ring and band cost only $830, so now it was almost paid for. I hoped it would be a nice surprise for them.

* * *

I handed the receipt to Dan when I arrived home.

"What's this?" He studied the piece of paper, then looked at me, confused. "I don't get it."

"Travis just bought you a ring. At least he was good for something."

"What do you mean?"

"I sold my ring to the store, got store credit, and applied it to your account. You owe me big time. I helped you find your wife, pulled your reception together, and almost paid off your ring." I playfully punched him in the arm. "Maybe it will help get your life started together."

"Wow, really?" Dan studied my expression for any hint of a joke.

"Yeah, seriously."

"Thanks, Sis," he whispered as he gave me a huge hug. "I know this has been hard on you, but we really appreciate everything you've done, and we couldn't have done it without you. This is the happiest I've seen you all summer."

He was right. I *had* been happy lately, and it was because I was busy. Busy helping other people. What I was doing was a good thing, and it made me feel good. Just like my mother had told me it would.

The ironic thing was it was something I'd thought I couldn't do. I'd thought it was too hard because this was a happy occasion for them and I was going to have to be happy. But what it did was force me to get over myself because it wasn't even about me.

"Okay, enough of the mushy stuff," I said. "We need to set up for your reception."

"Thanks," Dan said sincerely.

"You're welcome. I'm glad I could do it." And I really, truly meant it.

* * *

Justin, Gretchen, Ashlee, and I loaded everything we needed and headed over to the church to decorate.

I was able to get a parachute through Bradley Benson's friend's connection, and between that and the many strands of twinkle lights from the garage, I hoped we could make the reception as close to a fairy tale as possible.

Once the parachute was hanging from the ceiling, lined with lights, and the twinkle lights on the trees were turned on, I could already tell the result was going to be exactly what I had been hoping for: magical.

I got even more excited when the tablecloths were on and the centerpieces were in place. We turned one on just to see the effect, and the glittered vase with the light inside was beautiful. We set lights under the tablecloth of the center table and used different-sized boxes to give height and variety to the food display.

Justin and Gretchen went around setting battery tea lights on all the tables, while Ashlee spread the diamond table confetti around. I hung the strings of tulle and lights at each end of the gym and created a glowing backdrop. The last thing we did was arrange the engagement photos on the tables around the room. Amazingly it took less than two hours. We turned all the lights on and stepped back to admire our work.

"I love it," Ashlee whispered in awe.

"Do you think Rhonda will like how you've decorated for the reception?" Gretchen asked.

"If she doesn't like it, that could be the drama," I said.

"That's right. She likes the whole Disney thing. I remember she sang a song from *Pocahontas* for the ward talent show," Justin said.

I thought of Luke. That was the night that had started it all for us. I took a breath. "This is as close to a fairy-tale wedding as I could get. Hopefully it's good enough."

"Seems like you found your calling in life." Justin looked over at me. "I'm a guy, and *I* think this is awesome."

"It's perfect," Gretchen announced.

"You did good, Sophia," Ashlee said.

"We all did good," I said, pleased with the outcome. "We did really good."

"So should we take bets on whether there's going to be any drama tomorrow?" Gretchen said as we locked up the building.

"Let's hope not," I said. "But it's a wedding. Drama comes with the territory."

Chapter Twenty-Five
Wish Me Luck; I'm Gonna Need It

WHY RHONDA AND DAN CHOSE to get married in August in Las Vegas was beyond me. The average temperature was one hundred twelve. Temperatures had been known to peak at one hundred eighteen, sometimes one hundred twenty-two. That factor right there made for a very hot, uncomfortable wedding. But giving Rhonda the benefit of the doubt, she'd probably never experienced temperatures reaching such ridiculous highs, and it was most likely hard for her to imagine just how hot it really got. When I asked her about it when they were first engaged, Rhonda had not been dissuaded. "I've always wanted to get married in Vegas. It seems so romantic and exciting."

"Rhonda, you do realize getting married in the temple is not like getting married on the Strip. There aren't going to be the flashing neon lights and the Elvis impersonators and the showgirls with the feathered plumes."

"That's not really what I'm looking for. The city itself seems so alive with excitement."

"Oh, trust me. You don't have to get married in Vegas to have excitement at your wedding. Or drama. Drama seems to come with the territory."

I'd been able to tell by the look on her face that she didn't believe me. In fact, I was pretty sure she was thinking something along the lines of *Maybe at your wedding, but not at my mine.*

I hoped for her sake drama would not ensue.

The day of the wedding was a complete madhouse, as expected. I ended up being Rhonda's chauffeur, in her mother's minivan, no less, because none of her other bridesmaids knew their way around Vegas and Jean still had a lot of discomfort with her ribs. Getting nails and hair done (Ashlee claimed to be too nervous to be in charge of hair) and picking up flowers took all morning. Justin and Gretchen were in charge of watching Rhonda's nieces and nephews while everyone was getting ready, and they also volunteered to do it during the ceremony.

It all seemed straightforward enough, but emotions were running high and adrenaline running rampant, resulting in a frantic feel to the day.

We all piled into the cars and headed off to the temple in the early afternoon. I was happy for the drive to the temple since it seemed like it might be the only downtime I would get the rest of the day. Ashlee was uncharacteristically quiet, and Justin and Gretchen were in the backseat involved in their own little world of blooming love. It allowed me to also be in my own little world. I had done a lot of praying the night before because I needed answers. I owed Luke answers.

As I exited the highway, I noticed a billboard on the side of the road. It was an advertisement for seat-belt safety. It read, "If you are looking for a sign, here it is. You don't always get another chance."

Talk about being exactly what I needed. It was my sign, literally. This was my second chance. This was my do-over. Not just with Luke but with life.

As I thought about it, it occurred to me that maybe sometimes I had to give up something good for something better. Married life with Travis had been hard. Whether or not it would have gotten easier, I'd never know. Maybe instead of hanging on to my divorce as a bad thing, I should look at it as a blessing. Did I really want to be constantly dealing with Travis and all the many ways he'd given up on things when they'd gotten too hard? He'd given up on me and our marriage. If I didn't fix things with Luke, I'd be giving up on Luke, and that would be, well, stupid. Really, really stupid.

Because Luke wasn't Travis. *Luke. Wasn't. Travis.*

I had said it many times, but had I actually thought about what it meant or believed it?

I knew Luke was a way better guy than Travis would ever be. I kept expecting Luke to act like Travis, but he never did. He treated me better than Travis ever had, and we got along better than Travis and I had. Was I about to give it all up because I was afraid to move forward? What was there to be afraid of with Luke? He had a whole list of virtues. And I needed to add how amazingly patient he was with me. I didn't want to lose Luke, and I would unless I faced my fears. There was absolutely no reason *not* to move forward.

Because I loved Luke. I loved him.

It required one more leap of faith, which was scary since I was less than graceful in so many ways (like being mature) and might possibly stumble on this virtual jump.

Really? Could it be this easy to clear up my confusion?

I grabbed my phone, ready to call Luke right then, but then I glanced at Ashlee next to me and Gretchen and Justin in the backseat and decided to wait. This was a phone call I wanted to have in private.

Once we were at the temple, I excused myself and found a bench to sit on away from everyone else. I slowly dialed Luke's number and held my breath. A line of sweat trickled down my back, and I wiped my sweaty palms on my dress. This was it. This was my speak-now-or-forever-hold-my-peace moment. This was one of those moments when I hated being an adult. I had to own up to my behavior and make a decision. This situation was my own fault, and I knew it.

"Luke?" I asked breathlessly when he answered.

"Sophia?" He sounded confused.

I was out of reasons to put it off any longer. "I'm sorry, Luke. I'm so sorry." I didn't mean to, but I choked up.

"About?" He sounded guarded but said nothing more. He was probably waiting for me to fess up to my multitude of infractions.

What wasn't I sorry for? Everything was a mess, and it was because of me. "For this"—I pictured an abyss between us—"this mess I made. I don't want you to be upset with me."

He remained silent, so I kept going. I tried to gauge his reaction by listening closely but, of course, could glean nothing. I thought maybe this would be easier to do in person so I could read his expression and body language, but face-to-face apologies were terrifying. "I don't want to screw this up. I care so much about you. I don't want to screw *us* up, but that's exactly what I'm doing. I'm messing it up."

"Do you understand where I'm coming from?" He made no effort to hide the irritation in his voice.

I nodded. "I'm letting my baggage with Travis ruin everything with us."

"I want to feel like you're not always waiting for me to hurt you. I love you too much to ever do what Travis did to you."

"I want to let it go. I do."

"I can't do it for you. That's something you have to do. I'll be there for you, and I'll support you, but only you can let it go."

My chin quivered, and a tear escaped. Everything he was saying was true. "I know it."

"Sophia." His voice softened.

I swallowed hard against the lump in my throat. "What if it's me?" I said quietly.

He was silent for a moment. "I'm confused. I thought you just said it *was* you."

"Travis accused me of changing after we got married, and that's why he wasn't willing to work at it. And even though I know he was a quitter, I can't help but wonder if there was truth to his accusation." I sighed. "What if we got married, and it really was me and you left me too?" There. I'd finally said it—my worst fear. "What if I'm like a black widow?"

"You're going to kill me after we get married?"

"No, that's not the right analogy. Maybe it's the praying mantis?"

"Who eats the male after they mate?" Luke said.

"Maybe Dr. Jekyll and Mr. Hyde is what I mean."

I could hear the doubt in his voice. "You secretly turn into a monster at night?"

"Luke, I'm serious—"

"I know, but—"

"I'm not expecting anything from you. I just want you to know I'm sorry. And I'm asking you to forgive me."

"Sophia—"

"I don't expect you to automatically forgive me when I have hurt you. You don't have to answer right now."

"Honey, I just need to know that you're trying to leave the Travis stuff behind. I just need to know that you want to be here with me. I just want to know how you really feel. Not this, 'I care about you' stuff. You care about a pet."

"I want to be with you. Not with anyone else. I did yesterday, I do today, and I will tomorrow, and the day after that, and the next day after that, and for the rest of my life."

"That's all I need to know."

"I am really sorry," I whispered.

"I know," he whispered back. "Me too."

"I know there is more we need to talk about, but I'd really like to do that in person. Maybe I could drive down this weekend and visit again? You know, once all the wedding excitement is over."

"I'd love to see you."

I hiccupped in an attempt to laugh. "I promise I won't run away this time."

"As long as you promise."

So I swallowed my fear and answered. "I do," I said, knowing there was no turning back.

I was on an emotional high when I hung up with Luke. I felt like a weight I had been carrying for so long was now gone. Tomorrow I could drive to Luke's and do it. I could tell him I loved him, and I was ready to move forward.

I daydreamed about my return. I pictured myself speeding along in the car, driving as fast as I could to get there, hair blowing in the wind, armed with the knowledge that I could really tell him I loved him without a doubt. You know, like you see in the movies. Then we would run toward each other, dramatically throw ourselves into each other's arms, and declare our love.

I felt I could clear hurdles, even with how clumsy I was. It must have been all the adrenaline making me delusional, imagining the "moment" I could finally admit to Luke I was ready to talk about marriage. I knew it was going to be incredible. I was expecting no less than earth shattering.

But first I had to make it through my brother's wedding and reception. Then I could fulfill my daydream.

* * *

Rhonda looked like, well, a Disney princess. I can't say I was surprised. Her dress was big and puffy, and the skirt had several layers of tulle on the outside that puffed it out even more, and it was long enough to cover the walking cast she had on her ankle. I wouldn't have been surprised if Tinkerbell had flown by spreading magic fairy dust everywhere.

Compared to the crazy-busy morning we'd had, everything with the ceremony and the pictures went smoothly. My only complaint was how hot it was, and I wasn't even the one wearing the heavy wedding dress. But it was the smile on my brother's face that made tolerating the heat completely worth it. I was so happy for him and for both of them.

Justin, Gretchen, and I left the temple after pictures with the wedding party but before Rhonda and Dan were finished taking theirs—Ashlee chose to stay with Rhonda to help out with the pictures—and we headed to the stake center to make sure everything was ready for the reception. Cali came a little later to help get the food set out.

Cali came into the kitchen and hugged me. "It's beautiful out there."

"Thank you. I hope everything goes smoothly tonight," I said.

"I think everything is on schedule," Cali said. "There are some teenagers from the Young Women in charge of making sure the centerpieces are lit, the food is well-stocked, and the punch bowl is replenished. The photographer has someone setting up a photo booth outside that looks really cool. Have you seen it?"

I shook my head. "I didn't have much to do with the photographer. Now I'm curious."

I followed Cali outside to where the photo booth was being assembled. The background was a large chalkboard with "And They Lived Happily Ever After" written on it in chalk. Twinkle lights lined the edges.

"It's perfect," I said.

We went back inside to see how everything was coming along and if there were any final touches we needed to take care of. I sure hoped not because it had been a long day and I was ready to relax. Gretchen and Justin were already in the room, double-checking everything.

Rhonda walked in with Dan, and I was about to ask her what she thought when I heard her gasp. Then she started crying.

Her reaction was not what I'd expected. I thought for sure she would love it.

"Rhonda, I, uh . . ." I was at a loss for words. I fumbled, trying to think of something to say.

"It's perfect, Sophia! How did you do all this?"

"You like it?" I was still in shock from her initial reaction. Dan put his arm around me and gave me a small squeeze.

Rhonda dabbed her eyes. "It's even better than what I would have done."

Coming from Rhonda, that was a huge compliment, especially since she prided herself in her entertaining skills.

"Thank you." She hugged me so hard I thought I heard a rib crack.

"No. Thank you," I replied. Doing this for them had been a blessing. It had saved me from myself.

As much as I wanted to stay there and bask in the spotlight of success, I had to keep going to make sure everything was set before the guests started arriving.

I turned and almost walked into my parents.

"Sophia," My mom said. "It's incredible. You did such a fantastic job."

"You really did," my dad reiterated.

After a hug from each of them, I slipped away and got back to work.

I was finally able to sit down after all the formalities of the reception: the couple was announced; the cake was cut; and the bouquet was thrown, which I caught even though I was *not* trying—it landed on my lap when I tripped and fell backward trying to avoid the rush when all the girls made a grab at it. As I was savoring my moment of rest, my phone rang.

Luke's number came up on the display. My heart skipped a beat.

"Hello?" I answered.

"How's the reception?" he asked.

I glanced at the happy couple. "Everything turned out perfect. The only thing missing is you."

"Good thing I'm here, then."

I looked around, shocked. "What? Where?" I searched the room until my eyes rested on Luke standing in the doorway. I hung up and rushed over to him. "You came?" I asked, despite the obvious.

"I came," Luke said.

I flung my arms around him and hugged him. "I'm so glad."

"So it's a good thing?"

"Yes."

"I didn't want to miss your birthday."

I hadn't even thought about it being my birthday. "This is the best birthday present ever." I smiled at him. I was happy. This was me feeling happy. It had been such an elusive feeling for so long. It struck me hard that I could actually feel it again. I'd had to lose it to actually appreciate how good it felt. I was happy. "How did you get here so quickly?"

He cocked his head slightly. "I hung up with you this morning and decided I didn't want to wait until tomorrow. So I got in the car and drove up here."

It was sort of the same big, romantic gesture I was thinking of, except he came to me instead of the other way around. I wasn't complaining.

"But how did you know where the reception was?"

"I called Justin," he said. "You look pretty good for a girl who just got over the chicken pox. I would have come up if you needed me, you know."

"First of all, I felt terrible. Second, I looked disgusting. Third, I owed you a huge apology that I had yet to say. And fourth, I know you would have come if I had asked." I hesitated before continuing. "I know we have sort of agreed to not talk about a certain guy who will not be named, but I want you to know something."

"Is it good?" Luke was understandably suspicious.

"For you it is."

"Okay, then." He waited.

"When Travis and I were on our honeymoon, we both got the stomach flu—the gross, disgusting kind where you can't keep anything down or in, the unattractive kind that no one wants to experience ever, let alone on their honeymoon. It's not exactly something I ever wanted to tell anyone. I still don't find the humor in it, and it's been a year and a half."

"Okay. Why are you telling me now?"

"Because after Travis had it, I got it. I had taken care of him when he was sick. I got him drinks, cleaned up after him, and tried to make him feel better. When I came down with it three days later, he wouldn't even stay in the room. He left me alone because he said he couldn't stand the smell and couldn't listen to me retching. He didn't hold my hair back or bring me cool washcloths or do anything more than leave a Gatorade on the night table while he was out and about on the ship.

"My whole point is you care and he didn't. You were willing to drive up and take care of me despite what I had and what I looked like, and I appreciate it. So, just for the record, you are nothing like him."

"Well, of course I would take care of you no matter what because unlike him, I love you."

"Thank you," I said, leaning in to hug him. Hard.

After a moment, Luke motioned toward the dance floor. "Would you like to dance?"

"As long as you don't mind my tripping over my own feet."

"Impossible," he said and started dancing. "Just follow my lead."

"You're a good dancer," I commented as he led me smoothly around the floor.

"Thank you." He didn't meet my eyes.

"Are you blushing?" I asked, noticing a slight pink coloring his neck.

"No, no," Luke insisted, but he was obviously avoiding something.

"What? Can't I comment on your dancing abilities? You're the first guy I've ever danced with who seems to know how to do it."

He let go of my hand and tugged on his neckline.

"You're embarrassed."

"No, I'm not."

"Why are you embarrassed? Were you one of those guys who took ballroom dancing in the Wilk. and had to dance with a pretend partner? Or maybe you're a closet fan of the dance competition shows on TV."

He looked me in the eye. "Fine. I had to take dance."

"You *had* to take dance?" I raised my eyebrows.

"Yeah." He nodded his head. "In middle school. I made the mistake of signing up for it as an elective. I thought it would be easy. I had no idea I'd be in a class full of girls, all taller than me."

Huh. Interesting. "Couldn't you change electives the next year?"

"I could have, but the dance teacher took a liking to me, as in, I became her favorite student. She constantly reminded the girls that they got to dance with a *handsome* young man."

"I have to agree. You are handsome."

"But when you're twelve and your teacher is old, like forty, that's the most embarrassing thing in the world. And then she liked me so much, she wouldn't let me out of the class for seventh and eighth grade. It was a very painful period in my life and awkward."

There was nothing awkward about his hand firmly held at the small of my back. There was none of the high-school-bear-hug hold or arms on each other's shoulders swaying back and forth but going nowhere.

"What was it you wanted to tell me in person?" he whispered in my ear.

"Way to be direct."

He leaned away so he could look at me. "Hey. I drove all the way up here because I couldn't wait to hear it."

"So you want to make sure it was worth your while?" My face flushed. The lights might have been dim enough for Luke not to notice.

"Definitely."

"I think you will find it worth your while."

"Oh yeah?" His voice was nothing short of sexy.

"Yeah. Because there are some things that are better doing in person. And telling you I love you is something I wanted to do in person."

He stopped dancing. "You love me?"

"Yes." I nodded my head vigorously.

"So what changed your mind?"

I laughed. "I didn't need to change my mind. It was just something I had to come to terms with in my own time."

"You had to come to terms with being in love with me, huh?"

"Maybe that's not the best way to put it. I needed to admit to myself what I'd been feeling for a while and get over some of my hang ups."

He lifted his eyebrows. "Oh, so you've been harboring feelings of love for me for a while now?"

My blush deepened. "Yes, I . . ."

"I knew it," Luke said loudly to no one in particular. Then he pulled me close enough to whisper. "And I love you too, Soph." He leaned in and kissed me.

In the end, I had my moment. It was totally different from the moment I had envisioned though. In fact, it was way better.

When we broke apart, I noticed my mom staring at us, her mouth slightly ajar. Either she was appalled at my kissing Luke so passionately in public, or she was surprised to see him here.

I cleared my throat and changed the subject. "The wedding turned out nice."

He nodded and smiled. "The reception turned out nice too."

"I have to agree with you on that," I said. "And not any drama."

"Thank goodness."

"And I didn't trip and fall into the wedding cake."

He pulled me a little closer. "That would have provided entertainment."

I giggled. "Is that all I am to you? A provider of entertainment?" I pretended to be offended.

"You provide far more in my life than just some entertainment." His expression was completely serious. Without warning, I choked up. I wasn't even sure why my emotions went spontaneously crazy. I blinked my eyes quickly, trying to hide the tears that had sprung up.

"Hey, are you okay?" He looked down at me, trying to catch my eye.

I wouldn't meet his gaze. Instead, I hid against his shoulder. "Yeah. I'm better than okay."

I was thankful he didn't say anything more. It gave me a chance to rein in my emotions.

"Being at a wedding isn't making you sad, is it?" Luke asked.

I shook my head. "No, no, it's not that."

"Is it something? All of a sudden you got quiet."

I smiled at him. "I'm happy." I paused, then added, "I'm glad it's you I'm with now. As painful as everything has been with my divorce, I'm happy I got you out of it."

"I'm happy it's me too." He leaned down and kissed me. "You look beautiful."

"Well, thank you," I said, suddenly feeling bashful.

"I'd even go as far as to say you are the most beautiful girl in this whole room tonight."

My cheeks flushed a deeper shade of pink. "Don't let Dan hear you say that. He might think you're insulting his bride."

"But it's true, and I'm not in love with his bride."

I blushed some more.

"You know," he said as he pulled away, "we haven't had our picture taken at the photo booth yet. I bet there's not a line now. Let's go check it out. We need a picture to remember tonight."

"As if we could forget." I laughed. It had been a lot of work getting to this point.

Luke smiled at me and took my hand. "Proof so we never do forget."

Just as he'd predicted, there was not one person in the photo booth. "C'mon," Luke said. "Looks like we got it all to ourselves." He winked at me and led the way.

The photographer posed us in front of the backdrop and snapped a couple of pictures. He told us to wait there while he printed them.

Luke turned and faced me. His voice got quiet. "I've been thinking maybe we should change some things."

Change? Like what? "You're not breaking up with me, are you?" I felt panic rising in my throat. Hadn't I just finally told him I loved him? Hadn't we just been kissing?

He got a mischievous expression on his face. "Why would I ever do that?"

I swallowed hard. "I don't know." I thought a moment. "I'm too high maintenance?"

"No, you're not. It's nothing like that." A smile played at his lips.

"So what, then?"

"What do you think about Sophia James?"

My heart stopped. "What? Are you serious? Or joking?"

He took both of my hands in his. "Sophia James," he repeated. "I've been thinking about it, and I like the way it sounds. It sort of has a ring to it."

Was he . . . ? He wasn't . . . was he . . . ? "Sophia James?" I gulped. "As in Luke and Sophia James?"

"Yeah, as in Luke and Sophia James. What do you think?"

"I'm not quite sure." I paused. "You're serious?"

"Serious enough that I drove all the way up here to ask you."

"So you're completely serious?" I waited. This was really happening.

"Sophia, I have been in love with you from the first time we had Sunday dinner at your apartment. I have always known you are the one, and now I keep thinking it's time we do something about it. I have been waiting to give you this ring since you came to visit me."

My heart started racing as he got down on one knee and slipped a diamond eternity band on my finger. "Will you marry me, Sophia?"

I swallowed hard. "I don't know what to say."

Luke held my gaze. "How about yes?"

"Yes!" I said, hugging him tightly.

In the background, the photographer kept snapping pictures.

Chapter Twenty-Six

God's Course Correction

I woke up the next morning thinking *I'm engaged.* I looked at the delicate band on my finger to confirm it was true. Engaged. How weird was that? Definitely not what I saw in the plans a year ago when I was in this very bed in the depths of depression. Crazy how things changed so quickly.

And now . . . I was facing life again, about to be remarried, and I wanted to burst with happiness and throw up at the same time. Probably not a pretty combination or sight.

I didn't spend time languishing in bed over my change in relationship status, even though I was tired. After the reception was cleaned up and we were back home, Luke and I had shared our news. It made for a late night to what had already been a long day.

I dragged myself out of bed because church was bright and early at nine. With four extra people staying in the house, showers were going to be running cold quickly, so I wanted to jump in first. I scrambled for the bathroom, relieved to find the shower free, and despite the extra people, we somehow all made it to church on time.

I was busier daydreaming about my future life with Luke, wedding plans, and how life was changing in general than I was paying attention to the talks in sacrament meeting. Until the third speaker.

Her name was Katherine, and she had recently been baptized. As she told her conversion story, she said something profound that resonated with me. "Disaster is God's course correction. Having my whole life fall apart forced me to rethink everything. Having my life fall apart changed the direction of my life. I can look back now and realize that the Lord's hand was directing my life, and He was in the details."

Divorce had been my disaster. Disaster was God's course correction. As with the speaker, having my life fall apart totally changed my direction. Now I could see the blessing in the disaster. I wrote down the quote so I wouldn't forget. But how could I forget? It had been forged in my soul, and it helped me let go of a little more baggage left behind from Travis.

Life with Luke was going to be very different from life with Travis. Luke was so different from Travis in so many ways, but it wasn't just that. *I* was so different than I was when I'd married Travis. *I* was a different person a year and a half later. I traced over the words I had written down and realized how blessed I had been since That Day in April so long ago when Travis had announced he wanted a divorce. I looked down the pew at where my friends sat—Luke, Justin, Gretchen, and Ashlee. I had good friends, which I considered a blessing. So much in my life would have been different had I not experienced my course correction.

What I realized from all of this was sometimes blessings are years in the making. What seemed like a bad thing short term was really a good thing long term. Sometimes I couldn't see the good from the bad because I couldn't see beyond what I wanted, but I learned that the Lord didn't work on the instant-gratification plan. And that was okay. I'd take the delayed gratification over instant gratification because my life was better because of it. It also meant I got to have Luke. Even though I didn't believe in happily ever after, I did believe in working on it.

Epilogue
Nine Months Later . . .

A CAMERA FLASHED IN MY eyes, momentarily blinding me. I should have been expecting it, but it still caught me off guard. The cries rose from a murmur to certain cheers of happiness. I stopped to catch my breath, then looked at Luke, who was standing next to me, holding my hand.

"We did it, Sophia."

I smiled at him, still in awe. "There's no turning back now."

"There is no way I would ever want to turn back now," he said and kissed me on the lips.

Cheers and clapping started again from our friends and family, who surrounded us as we walked out of the San Diego Temple.

"Congratulations, you two!" Rhonda about bowled us over as she ran up to us. "You're married!"

"Thank you, Rhonda," Luke said.

She gripped her bouquet with one hand and held on to her bulging stomach with the other. She looked about ready to pop. I was afraid all this wedding excitement might put her into labor. "I never thought I would ever see you get married. I mean, I really was worried there for a while."

"Rhonda"—I put my hand on her shoulder—"you worried too much." Then I pulled her in and hugged her.

"Congratulations, sis," Dan said and hugged me. "And, Luke, I'm glad it's you she's married to." Dan shook Luke's hand.

My mom and dad came up to us next and hugged us both. "I am not going to know what to do with myself now that both of my kids are married," my mom said.

I knew that was an unlikely scenario since she was always in constant motion.

"I hope you two are planning to have kids right away," she continued.

"Nooo!" Luke and I said in unison and shook our heads. I looked over at Rhonda, with her hand on her back and Dan supporting her. "That's their job for now," I said.

"Welcome to the family!" Kay said, giving me a kiss on the cheek. She then turned to Luke and hugged him. "Congratulations."

Gretchen approached us, congratulated us, then asked me, "Do you know where you're going on your honeymoon yet?"

I shook my head, pushing my veil from my face. "Nope. No idea. But I'm sure it's not a cruise."

I pulled Luke in and kissed him.

After a few more minutes of visiting and taking some final pictures, we were at last alone, driving together to the reception.

"I love you," I said.

"I love you too."

"Thank you," I added.

Luke raised his eyebrows. "For what?"

"For waiting for me."

"Sophia"—he leaned over to kiss me—"you were worth waiting for."

About the Author

UNLIKE SOPHIA, SALLY JOHNSON IS not tall, blonde, or divorced. She grew up in Massachusetts and received her bachelor's degree in English from Brigham Young University. She and her husband, Steve, have four children and currently live in Las Vegas (but sadly not in a hotel). She has always had an overactive imagination and has finally found a way to put it to good use.